COMIC SANS

a novel

Katie Mlinek

Copyright © 2017 by Katie Mlinek

All rights reserved. No part of this publication may be reproduced or transmitted in any form or by any means, electronic or mechanical, including photocopy, recording, or any informational storage and retrieval system, without permission in writing from the author.

This is a work of fiction. Names, characters, businesses, places, and events are either the products of the author's imagination or are used in a fictitious manner. Any similarity to real persons, living or dead, or actual events is entirely coincidental.

Cover design by Flynn Walkinshaw

Printed by CreateSpace in the United States of America

ISBN-13: 978-1545190319

ISBN-10: 1545190313

For any questions or comments, please contact comicsansthenovel@gmail.com

Dedicated to Beth, Claire, Abbie, Lucy, and Ruth

> "O cursèd spite,
> That ever I was born to set it right!
> Nay, come, let's go together."
>
> — Shakespeare, HAMLET

Chapter 1

I'm a Comic Sans kind of person. I know. It's despicable. I didn't know it before but I do now, and knowing something for sure is nice, at least. Like knowing that you definitely can't stomach a ghost pepper or bike forty miles without passing out. And I learned all that stuff the hard way, if you want me to be honest.

I think everything I've learned has been through the hard way. I've learned that Mom will always think my favorite color is red. See, I used to think that rainbows were for ordering colors from best to worst, red being the best and violet being the worst. So as a kid I always said that red was my favorite, because I thought I'd be a fool to not like the best color.

I've learned that most people don't like pineapple on their pizza. That my dad can watch seven hours of *Ice Road Truckers* and eat two family-sized bags of Doritos and still not hate himself. That jobs are hard to get, easy to lose, and never pay enough.

The past year was tough, which you'll see soon enough. I guess you could say I learned a lot, or something sappy like that. Is there even an easy way to learn something? If there is, I probably don't want to know it. The hard way is always more fun.

Comic Sans

Chapter 2

I believe that there's an absolute truth to everything. I don't have time for this "relative" nonsense. *Hamlet* is unarguably fantastic literature, T-shirts are unarguably the best clothes. If you like apple juice better than orange juice, you're simply *wrong*.

That also means there's a right way to do something. See, I say quotes right, the way they're supposed to be read, so they sound natural. In my English class, everyone stumbles over the words like they're driving down a road full of potholes. It's always the worst readers who volunteer. The rest, the ones who can semi-read, don't even pay attention. Like Alicia Stai, who sits behind me in English, who's sat behind me in a total of six classes since freshman year, and who I know, without a doubt, does not pay attention — ever.

"James. James. James," Alicia said. She talked in a cliché white girl voice, vocal fry and all, always gossiping in an undertone to whoever would listen about the latest couples and breakups. She rolls her eyes so much that I'm surprised they haven't plopped right out of her head yet. She tapped me on the shoulder with her fingernail – a chipped purplish polish this week. I turned around and raised an eyebrow, not the flirty sort because I hate flirty eyebrow raises, but one that says, "Excuse me? What could you possibly want now?"

She giggled. Dang, the eyebrow raise might have seemed a little flirty. Alicia would flirt with a spork if she was bored, or at least with the very pen she was holding. I maybe wasn't the junior all the freshies wanted to date, but I was obviously on the same level as Alicia's pen.

"So I was wondering, about, you know, the project," she said.

"Mmhmm."

"How is Mrs. D going to grade our projects if we're done right before summer? Like, school will be over!" she said.

"Holy crap." I turned around in my seat to face her. "You –"

"Watterworth!" Mrs. Dessarollee was giving me a look from the front of the room. "Stop pestering Miss Stai and pay attention. You guys have a lot of work to get done and I'm trying to give you as much class time as possible. Okay everyone, extra copies of the rubric are up here. You can get into your groups and start researching."

I jumped from my seat and started dragging chairs to our group's computer against the wall. I glanced back at the class and saw that my group members were taking their good ol' time stretching and looking at the cheesy motivational posters around the room. The posters have been there all year. I know because I, too, have gotten distracted looking at them. They're like a car crash on the wall. One has a picture of a guy smiling really wide and the words "DO SOMETHING GREAT TODAY." But if you look really closely – which I did, once, after class when everyone had left – you can see a tiny piece of food stuck in his teeth. Like he forgot to floss or something. What a great accomplishment.

I've learned that my English class group will never exactly show passion for working, but other than that, they're okay.

Comic Sans

There's Veronica Kavka, who has never said a non-sarcastic thing in her life. Miranda acts like a fairy threw up on her and now she's confused about everything. Eleanor is the person who we all know will end up doing most of the work in the project. Mason is.... Well. I think his grandma is rich. And he has a really big nose. And I don't think he ever wore enough deodorant, and since we were getting closer to summer, and it was getting warmer, well, you just can't get away with that kind of stuff as a junior in high school. But he thinks he can.

While my group kept rubbernecking, I went ahead and pulled up some pages for research. Finally they all made it over to the computer.

"How much more do we have to do?" Mason asked. "I finished my part last night."

"Like the whole project, dummy," Veronica said.

"Parts? We had parts? What was my part?" Miranda asked.

"I don't remember anyone splitting anything into parts yet," Eleanor said.

"Well I sent a message to the group chat saying that I did the biography on Shakespeare," Mason said.

"There's a group chat?" Miranda asked.

"Did no one add Miranda?" Eleanor asked. She pulled out her phone and checked through the messages. "Huh. I don't think anyone did. What's your number?"

Miranda took Eleanor's phone and punched in her number.

"I really did send that message," Mason said to Veronica. "I finished it all last night. The whole thing."

"Like hell you did," Veronica said.

Katie Mlinek

"Guys!" I turned away from the computer and looked at them. "Does anyone have the rubric?"

Everyone looked at each other and then at me. They looked like meerkats, I swear.

"We have a group chat but no rubric?"

As everyone kept looking at each other, Eleanor started giggling.

"Alright, alright, hold on one second," she said, and grabbed five papers from the front of the room. She was still laughing a little as she came back. "Here you guys go," she said, handing each of us a paper. "Maybe *now* we can actually get started on this project."

"Not if the group chat stays in the state it's in," I said. Which is true. I don't think Mason is lying about sending that text, but the little group chat that Eleanor set up was so, I don't know, *hopping* that it's possible one small text got mixed up in all the rest. Last class, when we all got into our groups and exchanged phone numbers and everything, Eleanor set up the chat so that we could keep everything straight during the project. But instead we all just started talking. It was mostly me and Eleanor, to be honest. Eleanor said something about how I'm "such a monkey," so I saved a ton of pictures of ugly monkeys to my phone and sent them all to her last night, but then it made Veronica's phone shut down and she was really mad about it, and she spelled every word wrong in her rant which made it even more hilarious. It was a good moment. I was just sitting on my bed with my phone but I felt weirdly kinda happy. Even though I hardly know these kids.

"Let's just start researching or –" I began to say.

"– we can get all the pictures now!" Miranda said. "We've got *tons* of time to research. Here, look at this picture of Shakespeare with hipster glasses!" And so Miranda got everyone

Comic Sans

to gather around the computer as they scrolled through strangely edited pictures of Shakespeare. Eleanor and I just looked at each other and smiled.

She was a nice girl. She likes fonts, which we all figured out pretty quickly when the first thing she wanted to do when we started this project was choose the fonts for the PowerPoint and a matching background design. She reminded me of a rabbit, with her nose that was always a little bit pink. But it wasn't an analogy that fit her well enough. She deserved something better.

"Oh my gosh, guys, look," I said after reading over the rubric. "This has ClipArt."

They all looked at the rubric then withdrew, not reacting in any way. All except for Eleanor.

Wow!" she said, "I don't think I've seen this on a school paper since first grade."

"Neither have I," I said. I whistled. "Boy. This is taking me back. And now I can't take this project seriously. Count me out."

"Wow, what a loss to our team," Eleanor said with a grin that she couldn't stop. We both looked at each other and smiled wide.

Katie Mlinek

Chapter 3

Dad said that cursing was for people too stupid to think of other words. I've heard him curse before, but only three times. Once was when he was driving his truck and he let me come along with him, like a cheesy father-son road trip. It was snowing so hard that I had stopped trying to see out of the windshield. Dad cursed when he thought he hit something, but it ended up just being trash on the road.

I can't imagine that he dreamed of being a truck driver, but he didn't go to college so he didn't have many options. He says that he didn't need it, seeing as people went off to college just to buy expensive books and listen to professors talk about how important it was to read the book. He says that almost every American who's achieved their dreams didn't go to college. I'm pretty sure Kim Kardashian isn't the best example of that, but it's the only one Dad could think of when I asked him. I bet the amount of times she's cursed in uncountable.

Another time he cursed was when he got a phone call during dinner. I can't actually remember what we were eating but I like to think that it was a quiche. The phone rang and Dad made all these smooth remarks about not wanting to leave such a beautiful quiche and then he got on the phone and was all silent a bit before cursing. Mom, when she's nervous, folds her napkin into a tiny little square and dabs her mouth, and she did that so much that she wiped off all her lipstick. I didn't even know she was wearing lipstick before. When Dad got off the phone, Mom started curling her napkin into a tight little ball and squeezing and releasing it again and again and asked if he was alright and he just shook his head, looking down at his quiche. Or maybe it was shepherd's pie. We went to a funeral a few days later for someone I didn't know. I was really young, but I remember seeing him in the casket, his face all powdery white like he'd been scared to death. Mom said that Dad had a dad, that everyone had a dad, but not everyone's dad is a good one. I didn't get that then, but I do now. My grandfather must have been an asshole. There, cursing like Dad.

The third time he cursed was today.

I got home from school and he came out of the living room to say hi and stubbed his toe on the doorframe and let out a whopper of a word, which seemed weird for just stubbing a toe. I asked if he was okay and he said, "Yeah, just fine," waving me off. He paused a moment. "Actually, no, sit down."

So I sat down and started running everything I'd done in the past month through my head, thinking he was going to chew me up for something, but I wasn't *that* bad a kid, and how could he know about me having a C in math? So he sat down across from me and patted my knee all awkwardly, like some real sweet scene from a Hallmark movie, only I thought it was annoying.

"I lost my job," he finally said.

I waited a second to see if he would say anything else. He didn't. "I'm sorry, Dad."

"It's not your fault."

"I know."

"It's not anyone's fault."

"Well, someone fired you."

Katie Mlinek

"Yes. But it wasn't their fault. James?"

"I'm sorry, Dad."

"No, listen. I want you to finish high school, okay?"

"Well, yeah."

"I mean, really finish it. Not barely finish it. But you don't have to be one of those top-of-the-class people either."

"Sure."

"You can't get a job anymore with just a scraped-together high school diploma. It wasn't that way when I was your age."

"I'm sorry, Dad."

"I know. It's not your fault. Companies just don't know who they're looking for."

"You'll find another job though, right? And there's severance pay and stuff, so we're good. Right?"

"Right." He got up and patted my shoulder this time, twice, pausing at the door for a moment before leaving the room.

Comic Sans

Chapter 4

The more I talked to Eleanor, the prettier she seemed. It's not like I never talked to her or noticed her, I just never *really* considered anyone named Eleanor having much of a personality. Don't give me the example of Eleanor Roosevelt – I've already tried to figure that one out. Eleanor's smart. Not just academically, though she's working on being president of the student council, but she seems like she has life all figured out.

We were already texting all the time. It's kind of tough, in a group chat, to have a conversation with just one person without annoying everyone else. But I didn't care much. I started to jump a little in excitement whenever I heard my phone go off. Sometimes it was just Miranda sending heart emojis for no real reason, or Mason trying to be sarcastic and funny. Even Veronica pitched in at times in surprising ways. She told us once about how her mom left her in the grocery store parking lot but never came back for her. Instead, her older brother had been driving by with some friends and saw her there and picked her up. And apparently it's the same plot as an episode of "Good in the Hood," the big sitcom these days. We all thought it was hilarious.

You know, there's never anything on TV until I have a lot of homework to do and suddenly everything's interesting. Even the old infomercials are interesting, just because it's a hoot to make fun of those disembodied voices. Sometimes, especially late at night when the crew and host are tired, I can get a glimpse of their hand when the camera's all wrong. One time I even heard the host chewing potato chips. Right next to his mic, stuffing himself with potato chips. Then he set down the bag in front of the camera and I saw that it was salt and vinegar, which is even worse 'cause the smell of that would stick to the mic for weeks. Imagine that, being surrounded by the smell of vinegar every time you have to work a dump job like that.

My mom doesn't have a job. She says she's a full-time mother and sure, she used to be, but I don't need 24/7 attention anymore, and I haven't been getting it for years at this point anyways. She's still involved in my elementary school PTA. *Elementary school.* She talks about getting a retail job but never ends up getting one. Now that Dad lost his job, though…. Well, I doubt anything will change.

It's been weird having him around the house more. He was an over-the-road trucker, which means he would be gone for two weeks at a time, driving to Oregon or Texas or even Canada. He made more money that way, apparently. With him being around more now, I can see the impact he's having on the house. Nothing's in the places I'm used to finding them in. Like just now, I tried to find a big bag of dill pickle chips and they were under the sink, along with the rest of our last batch of groceries. Who puts food in a place like that?

I sat down in front of the TV and started eating them. They're the best kind. I mostly like them because Mom and Dad don't, so I never have to worry about them eating it while I'm gone at school or something. Mom came into the living room and sat down on a couch and started watching TV with me. I like that sort of stuff. Just sitting in a room with someone without talking. Whenever Dad would get back from his long weeks away, Mom would talk to him for *hours.* I swear, she told him every thought she had over the past two weeks. But I like to just sit in the same room with him quietly and listen to the radio or something. Mom can't sit in silence for long, though.

Comic Sans

"The neighborhood block party is later today, and I want you to wash your nice pair of khakis for it," Mom said.

"Why can't I just wear regular shorts?" I asked.

"I want you to look presentable, that's all," she said. "And it's going to be different this time, since there's all those new people."

That is true. We have around two block parties a year – one towards the beginning of school and one towards the end. Last time, though, they had just started building all these brand new, fancy houses down the road from ours, and people started moving in just two months ago. So I guess they're invited and considered a part of the neighborhood now. It's weird, though. These are houses with circle driveways and well-groomed shrubs and one of them even has a stone birdbath. Next to our ramshackle houses, they don't really fit. Our steps don't even have a railing, so we don't use it in winter when it's too icy. Once, when there had been a particularly bad ice storm, I even saw Mom climbing up the little hill to our door on all fours. These people probably have professional ice melters come to their house or something. If that's even a thing.

"Do I have to go?" I asked.

"Yes."

"Are you making red velvet cupcakes again?"

She nodded. She's prized for her red velvet cupcakes. There was really no point in me asking, anyways, because she's made them for every single block party since I was seven, when she "hit it big" with them. I swear, some of the neighbors only say hi to me because they want her to bake them some red velvet cupcakes. She does sometimes, for Christmas and stuff like that as presents.

My phone buzzed again and I checked it just as the commercials were ending. It was Eleanor, responding to

Katie Mlinek

something Miranda had just said. I smiled as I tried to think of something witty to add.

"Do kids even text *that* much?" Mom asked. "I mean, you all see each other in school every day."

"Yeah, Mom. Everyone texts all the time."

"Hmm. Hand me the remote."

I tossed it over to her while still looking down at my phone, and she changed the channel to TLC. I looked up.

"Seriously, Mom?" It was some show about ex-convicts getting married.

"What?" she said. "You weren't watching anything."

"Yeah, but this is garbage."

Dad walked into the room. "There you are," Mom said. She turned the TV off with a click. Dad sat down on the couch next to her. They both looked at each other. And that's when I knew: this was going to be a "talk." We've already had sex talks before, and drug talks, and "we still love you even though you're growing up" talks. So what could this be about?

"Listen, James," Dad began. I braced myself. "You know I've just lost my job and all."

"Right."

"Well, your mother and I have been talking about finding ways to pay off bills, just for this month. Who knows how long I'll be out of a job, hopefully not long. But we've decided…." He broke off and looked at Mom. "We figured canceling the phone bills would be the easiest thing to do. Just for this month! This won't be forever. Your mom and I, we aren't going to be using our cellphones, either. We'll just have the landline. For now."

Comic Sans

"Oh," I said. I looked down at my phone just as another text from Eleanor popped up. "Okay."

"Alright?" Dad said. I looked up at Mom and Dad. I didn't want them to see how disappointed I was. I think Mom knew, though. She always does somehow.

"Yeah," I said, "alright."

"Atta boy." Dad got up, slapped me on the shoulder, then left the room. Mom and I sat in silence in the living room for a moment. She didn't say anything, and I didn't, either.

"Well," I said. I slid my phone over the coffee table to her. "I think I'll go ride my bike."

"Okay," she said, still giving me that sympathetic look. It drove me crazy. I didn't want to see it anymore. I wanted nothing to do with it.

Katie Mlinek

Chapter 5

I got my bike out of the garage and jumped on. It was really a nice day but I was having a hard time appreciating that sort of thing all of a sudden. I steered down Poplar Avenue and took the first right.

This must be where the block party is going to be. One of my neighbors (a bald but bearded weirdo who's name I've never known but who I've always referred to in my head as "Beard-o") was setting up tables with tablecloths and weighing it down with books to keep them from blowing away. I turned down the next road and biked even faster. I felt all of this rush, I don't know what for, but I felt like I had to do something, or go somewhere. So I just kept biking.

Normally, I love riding my bike. I do it all the time. I know this may sound strange, but my favorite part of biking is feeling the wind underneath my armpits. It's such a cool, pleasant feeling, being freed of my oppressive underarm sweat. But you just can't say that sort of thing to people. I tell everyone I like to bike just for fun and no one ever asks questions beyond there. I'll probably end up biking more, now that I can't text anyone ever. I guess I need to get into better shape anyways, with all those dill pickle chips I eat. But how are Mom and Dad going to communicate with people, now that their phone bills will be cancelled, too? The only calls we get to our landline are telemarketers or people asking for donations.

Comic Sans

This seems pretty quick and impulsive, if you ask me. I mean, it's the beginning of May so the month has already begun. Don't we still have to pay the bill? Is that how it works? And how does Dad expect to get a new job without a cellphone? I don't know. I don't know any of this stuff.

I turned onto Windsor Street and biked past all the brand-spanking-new houses. The one with the birdbath had just gotten its grass cut, I could tell. That house is ridiculous. I swear, they cut the grass two days ago. *Two days.*

You know, cellphone or no, Dad will probably get a job soon anyways. No use being angry about everything. I mean this is all so sudden, and it's temporary, right? But you know what, *I* could get a job, maybe pay for my phone bill myself or something like that. I mean, summer is almost coming up and I guess everyone gets to the point in high school when they ought to have a summer job. I could maybe offer to cut the grass for these houses, get a couple extra bucks here and there. At least I know it would be a regular job.

I turned onto Edmunson Street and there was Mrs. Cobbleson, the local neighborhood nut. I nodded. She always introduced herself to everyone as Delilah T. Cobbleson, and she had these giant glasses that magnified her eyes, so she seemed like she was always in a permanent state of wonder.

I don't like going past her on my bike. It makes me sort of nervous. She doesn't always just do a nice nod and wave like most people. She walks up to you as you bike towards her where you have no choice but to stop, and she always invites everyone over for tea. I feel bad having to say no, but I always do. She's not nutty *all* the time, though. It's like a mood thing. You know she's perfectly fine and sane if she just waves at you from a distance. Mom says she used to babysit me all the time. I don't remember any of it.

Katie Mlinek

Everyone knows about her, though. Mom said that her husband died a couple of years ago from cancer, and she has no kids, and she had been a nurse in the Vietnam War and that's when she lost it, but it was her husband dying that really sent her over the edge. It makes me sad, but there's nothing I can do about it.

I pretended like I just forgot something and circled around and to bike back to the house, just so I wouldn't have to talk to her. I really didn't feel like biking anymore. And as I biked back, I saw other neighbors already getting together at Beard-o's house, setting up rolls and pickles and brownies and stuff. A few of them waved and I nodded. I started biking a little faster so I could get home in time to take a shower before going. I sweat like a sumo wrestler, I really do. Mom hates it. Sometimes she makes this big fuss about not giving me a hug before bed because I'm so gross and sweaty, and pretends like she's really denying me something valuable. I think it bugs her more than it bugs me, though. It doesn't bug me one bit. Part of me thinks that she *wants* me to get upset. I'm almost a grown man, I don't need bedtime hugs. But whatever.

I got home and took a shower and even combed my hair for the block party. I could smell Mom's fresh red velvet cupcakes the whole time. When I got downstairs, she had just finished icing them.

"C'mere, James, carry these for me," she said, handing me a full platter of cupcakes. She brushed her hands on her apron and scurried to the bottom of the stairs. "Hurry up, David!" she hollered.

She tore off her apron with gusto and started frantically applying makeup in front of the little mirror we have at the bottom of the stairs. "David!" she shouted again. I heard a feeble cry from Dad upstairs and finally he came down.

"How does my hair look?" she asked him.

Comic Sans

"Fine. Really nice. You got the cupcakes? Okay, let's go."

We set off, me holding the cupcakes and Mom and Dad leading the way. Right before we turned the corner of Poplar Avenue, Mom turned and took a good look at me.

"Do you have those cupcakes okay? Wait, where are your khakis? I told you to wash them."

I looked down as if just noticing that I was even wearing pants at all. "Sorry, Mom, I forgot," I said. She huffed and kept walking.

Most of the entire neighborhood was there already. All in all, probably around one hundred people. It's really a pretty large neighborhood, and the block party is way more than just one block of houses. There were cheers as I brought the red velvet cupcakes over to the table.

And that's when the awkwardness began. There really aren't any kids my age in the whole neighborhood. There are kids just slightly older, freshman and sophomores back from college already, and kids slightly younger by two or three years, but none quite around my age for me to feel comfortable talking to them. Adolescence is weird this way. When you're a little kid playing in a park, it doesn't matter if you're two or five, and then once you're old, it doesn't matter if you're fifty or sixty, you can be friends no problem. But there's a huge difference between twelve and sixteen that just makes things, well, awkward.

I recognized most of the people that were there, but there were always people I didn't know. There was one guy who used to be really good at balloon animals, just as a hobby, you know, and at all the block parties he would make us whatever balloon animal we asked for. Then he moved away. He was the best, though.

I saw Mrs. Cobbleson again. She must actually be pretty sane today, because she was surveying someone's garden and giving them advice. In the center of it all, everyone was cooing

Katie Mlinek

over some new baby named Hollie, which I've never understood since babies are pretty ugly and they frown more than they smile. I saw a guy named Ben, or at least I think his name is Ben. He likes to bike a lot, too, but he's a little more intense about it than I am. I see him going in and out of the neighborhood on his bike sometimes in one of those tight exercise sort of shirts and it reads "BEN" in giant, reflective letters on the back. So that's why I think his name is Ben.

Mom goes crazy at stuff like this. She had already dragged Dad through probably twenty conversations by the time I had made it over to the food table. I didn't see anyone with plates of food yet, but I was so awkward that I didn't know what else to do but get food. It's easier to stand around feeling uncomfortable with a plate in your hands than with nothing for your hands to do.

The second I got a plate, though, people started lining up behind me. I guess I started dinner without even realizing it. Two women who I think I had seen before, but didn't know, were talking next to me.

"Yeah, I heard he was fired just a couple of days ago," the taller one said.

"Everyone's getting fired, hon. I'm just glad they can afford to get all the ingredients for those cupcakes still. Otherwise, I'd be losing it."

I perked up and took a better look at the two women. They had to be talking about Dad, right? I'm not just being paranoid? I kept listening as I piled food on my plate at random. How could they have heard?

"I think he was either a trucker or a mailman or something like that, so it's not like he could have been making good money," the taller one said.

"Trucker," I whispered through grit teeth.

Comic Sans

The shorter one was squat, with a round face and giant gold hoop earrings that squished against her neck, they were so big. "No one's making good money 'round here, baby doll," she drawled.

I skipped over the salad at the end of the table and stomped off to eat underneath a tree. I watched the two women as they laughed together. Never mind how empty-headed they must both be. How did they know so much? We keep a pretty low profile in the neighborhood, more or less. I guess I ought to have known there was some sort of gossip circle in place, but we should have been entirely clear of something like that.

What made me most mad, though, was that all they cared about was how it affected them and their red velvet cupcakes. I mean, here I've already lost my phone and who knows what else will come soon, but it's just talk on their side, their sniveling, stupid, toadstool conversation with their neck fat and –

"James?" I looked up and there, as if descending from the clouds above, was Eleanor. I'm being serious, I think the clouds parted and sun rays zoomed over to us the second she said my name.

"Woah, Eleanor! What are you doing here?" I asked.

"Well I, you know, *live* here," she said.

"What?" How could I have not known this? I've been living here since I was three – I would have known if there was someone else my age by now.

"Yeah, I live in one of those new houses. We just moved in around two months ago," she said.

"Really? That's so awesome! I can't believe we live in the same neighborhood! I biked past there just earlier today. Which house do you live in?" I probably should have known that she lived in that section. I don't know why, but it just made sense that

Katie Mlinek

she'd be relatively rich. Suddenly, it occurred to me that she might have heard about Dad being fired, and for some reason I really didn't want her to know.

"I live in the house with the red door," she said.

I raised my eyebrow.

I shook my head. How am I supposed to recognize a house based on a door?

"The one with the bird bath," she said.

"Oh," I said, "yeah, I know that one." Inside, I felt like screaming with laughter. What a coincidence! Eleanor, of all people, living in that wretched bird bath house. Inside, I was bubbling over with repressed laughter, like when you shake up a soda while the cap is still on, though outside I was just an awkward guy who was saying nothing. We stayed there like that for a moment, just under the tree. Standing. Not really looking at each other. "Wanna sit down and eat?" I asked.

She nodded and we sat down on the tree roots. They kind of hurt a little bit, but the only place to move would be closer to her and I just feel like that would have been awkward. Like, maybe she would have thought that I was trying to get closer to her or something when really I just didn't want a tree root kicking my butt all day long.

"Hey," she said, "did you see that picture Veronica sent? To the group chat? Wasn't that hilarious?"

I had just taken a giant bite of pulled pork and had to swallow it quick. "Picture? I don't think so. I haven't, uh, checked my phone since this morning. I've been busy. Biking and, you know, getting ready for this and stuff." I gestured to the block party.

She nodded. "Cool."

Comic Sans

We kept eating and looking around at everything. It was silent again and a little weird. Over text, we can talk back and forth without a pause for hours at a time. But in person, it's just…I don't know, *different*.

She took a bite of a red velvet cupcake. "Woah!" she said through a mouthful. "Where did this come from? This is the best cupcake I've ever had. I'm liking this neighborhood more and more."

I laughed. "My mom made that, actually," I said.

"Seriously? Can I come over someday so she can teach me how to make something like this?"

"Yeah, that would be awesome," I said. I knew she was joking but already I was thinking in my head how great that would be. Her and my mom bonding in our kitchen over flour and red food dye. It would be a nice moment. If something like that ever happened.

"My parents made me take a baking class for a while," Eleanor said, "but I hated it. It was terrible. Once, I faked being sick so that I wouldn't have to go. But my parents still made me. I'm the worst baker you'll ever meet. Truly. I've never even faked being sick to get out of school, and I wasted my one go at it."

I sat up straighter. "What? Your parents *forced* you to go to a baking class? Why? That's insane."

She nodded. "Yeah. I don't know, my dad thought it was important for me to be a 'well-bred lady,' as he put it. I think it was a little over-hyped. I don't know. They just want me to do things like that sometimes and normally it doesn't hurt, I kind of like dabbling in different stuff. But I was just really bad at baking. And everyone else there was so good and, well, it's not like I was super *self-conscious*, that's not it, I just didn't enjoy it. It was tedious. Measuring out every ounce of flour and things like that."

Katie Mlinek

I nodded. "I don't think I've ever baked or cooked anything in my life. You're probably still way better than me."

She laughed. "I don't know about that, you should see my mac-n-cheese. I burn it every time, somehow. Even Velveeta, which is my favorite kind. I know it's really bad and cheap, and my parents only get it the day before Thanksgiving every year when all the other food in the house is being prepped for Thanksgiving dinner. They get really meticulous about every dish being perfect and timed right and hitting the exact correct temperature. It's a little exhausting. I'm glad I don't have to do it. I like the night before better, with nothing but crappy Velveeta."

"Dude, Velveeta is great. But c'mon, the day *after* Thanksgiving is way better. You get to eat leftovers all day long while your parents are gone Black-Friday-shopping their lives away," I said. But wait, did I just call her "dude?" What's wrong with me? What part of my brain is completely broken today? And that's when I realized that over text I call her "dude" all the time. Ugh. So my brain is *constantly* broken.

She laughed again, though, so hard she almost dropped her plate. But after that, we both just…fizzled out. Again. You know when you're having a great conversation with someone but then you just run out of things to say and you both sort of look at the ground, each desperately thinking of something to say? Well, that happened. I could tell she was a little stressed about thinking of something to say, too, until she was the first one to lift her head and start up something new.

"You know, Mason is like the Impact font," Eleanor said.

I laughed. "I have no idea what that means, but I can still sort of see it."

"It's the one that's really bold and hard-edged and in-your-face. Like the words are slamming against your face as you read it. An actual impact," she said. "Which is kind of like Mason."

Comic Sans

I laughed again. "You *really* like fonts, huh?"

She nodded. "I like to handwrite them, too. I make little illustrations and write quotes around them and put them all over the wall in my closet. My parents won't let me put them up in my actual room, but I like my closet. It's cozier in there."

"Wow, that's not something you hear every day," I said. "Most people who are banned to their closets are oppressed and also a Disney princess."

Eleanor laughed. "How do you even know about Disney princesses? You're an only child, right?"

I nodded. "Yeah. I mean, I know I live under a rock and all, but I hand out candy on Halloween in our neighborhood and trust me, I've seen every version of Cinderella there is."

Just then, a tall man and woman walked over to us. The woman had her hair up all fancy and the man was wearing a navy blue suit. He didn't look uncomfortable at all, though – and this was not suit weather.

"Ellie, we're going to get going now," the man said. He turned and nodded at me. I stood up – I felt like I was supposed to do something, but what, I don't know.

"We just got here, Dad," Eleanor said. She looked over at me as if I was going to agree with her. But I just kept standing there. I mean, I can't take sides in something like this.

"We really need to be getting back," the woman, presumably Eleanor's mom, said. Her parents kept looking at me. The whole situation felt weird. So I decided to just go ahead and introduce myself. I held out a hand to Eleanor's father.

"My name is James. I live right around the corner," I said. "Well, and a couple of streets down. On Poplar Avenue."

Katie Mlinek

He shook my hand. "Nice to meet you, *James*." He said my name strange, like he was trying to memorize it or something. "My name is Alex, and this is my wife, Diane," he said.

I nodded at her. This is doubly weird, now. I can't call these fifty year old people Alex and Diane! And there was something so *formal* about this that I felt like I wasn't even in my neighborhood anymore. I was holding a paper plate covered in pulled pork and I probably had some in my teeth and my shoes were second-hand. Who didn't belong, them or me?

"Let me just throw away my plate real quick," Eleanor said. She left us underneath the tree as she walked over to a trash can. Her parents didn't move.

"She, uh, Eleanor told me about those baking classes," I said. "Where were they? It sounded fantastic. Really fantastic." Hey, someone had to make conversation.

"In the city," her dad said. "They were with Chef Erin Vergelli." He looked at me expectantly.

"Oh, that's very…nice," I said.

"Ever heard of Chef Vergelli? She's the one that owns Bella Italiana. Michelin star. I've been looking into her cooking classes for Ellie, too, since she enjoyed the baking one so much."

I nodded and smiled, unsure of what to say, but thankfully Eleanor came back just then.

"Ready to go, Ellie? Alright. Well, very nice to meet you, James," her dad said. Eleanor gave a meek wave and with that, they left.

It's interesting that they call her Ellie. It's nice, a nickname like that. Am I not supposed to call her Eleanor? Well, it has to be fine – everyone at school calls her Eleanor. But you know, I really like Ellie. It's so personal and quaint (oh gosh, I sound like

Comic Sans

Mrs. Cobbleson), but it feels so relaxed compared to *Alex and Diane*. I wonder if only the people closest to her get to call her Ellie. Like it's an exclusive club or something. I wonder if *I'll* ever get to call her Ellie. But I can only ever be James. Can't get much shorter than that – *or* more interesting.

Chapter 6

At the dinner table the next night, Mom and Dad announced that we were going to wash the dishes from now on – no more dishwasher. It's only been a little over a week but Dad calculated how much water from the dishwasher costs versus just washing the dishes, and apparently it's enough for it to be worth us not using it for a while. I don't know why they keep talking about all these changes being temporary. I'm starting to wonder if they are at all. I mean, they've very quickly started cutting back on everything, and they act as if they're barely cutbacks at all. Like they can fool me into thinking we're not struggling for money immediately. I'm not five anymore. Does anyone here realize that?

But it made me think that I need to stop procrastinating and just get a job already. I told this to Mom, and she thought it was a great idea. She said there were tons of places hiring this time of year and that I ought to look now before people start taking them.

So I got my resume all ready for Mom to look over. I sat on the couch just looking at speck of dirt in the carpet while I waited for her, wishing more than anything that I could time travel into the future just a little bit. See, she was doing her monthly jewelry cleaning. She has a huge collection of jewelry stretching back to when she was six years old. She lost all of her pictures, almost every single one except for a handful, in a basement fire in her house while she was gone at college. So she started to consider her jewelry as snapshots of her life instead. There's a pair of earrings

Comic Sans

that she wore throughout most of elementary school, a pair she wore to her first dance in middle school, a pair that her grandma gave her when she got her tonsils out, stuff like that. And every month she polishes all of them. It's just something I've come to accept over the years. Though I don't fully understand it, I can see how important it is to her. She has a little ritual for polishing them. She sits down at her dresser and goes through them all one by one, turning on a radio station that only plays fuzzy classic rock. She always lets us know if it's going to be a polishing day, and Dad and I tease her endlessly for it because there's really no reason to polish them all that much, they just seem like hunks of metal to me. But she always does it with the same seriousness each time.

 When Mom was finally finished, she scrolled through the resume so quick I wondered if she was even reading it at all. When I was writing it, I realized how little I had done with my life. I know that sounds depressing and all, but it didn't really depress me that much. I'm just not that into planting trees in parks or giving my blood everywhere I go or stuff like that. So I just beefed up the resume a little more than it should really be, adding a few extra words to awards I had gotten in middle school to make it sound fancier, maybe an acronym here or there, the like. Mom gave it the "a-okay" so I went ahead and started the job search. I had seen a "FOR HIRE" sign in the windows of both The Dollar Tree and Food Lion, which are all in the same shopping center so I can hopefully get both interviews done on the same day. Mom had the phone number to Smith's Gastro Pub, but I couldn't get the interview for two weeks. That seemed weird to me. I mean, it's a pretty hopping restaurant, and it's British food (who knew British food was its own thing?), so it's relatively high class, but that just seemed like a long time. I don't know. I've never done this before.

 I told Eleanor about this job thing, minus the whole resume part, and she thought it was great. I partly wanted her to know just because she's always doing interviews for different

Katie Mlinek

organizations and leadership positions and things like that, and whenever she asks what I've been up to, I don't really have anything to say back.

    Miranda said her cousin used to work at Smith's Gastro Pub and the pay is good, real good. Like ten bucks an hour good, plus tips, which is weirdly a lot for a restaurant. And of course, compared to the minimum wage at Dollar Tree, it's great. Way more sophisticated than a low-class job in a store full of chemically-engineered junk. But hey, at least I don't have to interview for some job as an infomercial host.

    Eleanor was saying something the other day about how she hates the smell of the Dollar Tree. I can't say that I smell it that often, or even go inside, but she swears that she can catch a whiff of it if she's walking past one. She says it smells like plastic and Ring Pops, which got her all distracted by her childhood that was apparently full of Ring Pops. But I didn't forget the plastic smelling part. It particularly struck me because I always thought my first grade classroom smelled like plastic.

    I have this one really specific memory of walking into that classroom and running to "The Rug." It was this big, cheap floor mat with different colored squares and every student got their own square, right, except this kid Brett kept taking my spot for no reason. That's why I ran to it, so he wouldn't take my spot for Morning Madness, a game we played every morning recapping what we learned in class the day before. So anyways, I remember sitting on my yellow square, thinking how plastic everything smelled. That's it.

    I know it's a really insignificant memory, and it doesn't mean anything to anyone but me. But now that smell – that plastic "Dollar Tree smell" – takes me back to the floor mat in that first grade classroom instantly. It's weird, nostalgia. I guess I understand Eleanor with the whole Ring Pop thing. It's like you can actually be in a different time and place, just thinking about

Comic Sans

strong memories like that. Maybe the closest we'll ever get to time travel is in our own heads. I don't know. Like I said, it's weird.

Katie Mlinek

Chapter 7

You know what else is pretty weird? My school. Then again, I'm sure everyone thinks their high school is pretty weird. Ours has triangle windows in the cafeteria, though. I mean, you can't get much weirder than that.

We have strict hallway rules. I guess things used to get pretty rowdy in the halls until they started cracking down, but this was all before I got here so it seems like hogwash to me. At least it's not like middle school, where you had to use your binder as a shield anytime you left a classroom. But anyways, the rules are really strange. Like, for instance, anytime you need to leave class to go somewhere other than the bathroom, you have to have a buddy with you. And they have this red line down the center of every hallway and you have to stay on the right side, unless you're crossing to go into a class on the left or something. I mean, no one really follows the rule unless Mr. Zanders, our principal, is there. Sometimes he stands in hallways looking all stern and scary and stuff and *then* everyone stays to the right side of the hallway. Once, a kid saw his friend on the other side and ran over to talk to him, and Mr. Zanders gave him in-school detention for a *week*.

Eleanor never crosses the line. Ever. As freshmen, we were all scared of crossing the line, but we didn't care so much anymore after maybe two months. But it's been three years now, and Eleanor still never does. I know because I see her once a day on

Comic Sans

the stairs between my Algebra II and Intro to Physics class, and at first she never saw me because she never looks up. She's always looking down, watching her feet, even though she knows exactly where they're going. I waited for a really long time to make eye contact on those stairs.

Then, one day, we finally did. But it's because I was wearing a clown nose, and who wouldn't notice something like that? We had been doing all this stuff measuring and graphing the curve of this clown nose my teacher brought into class, and when it was my turn to go up to the board I put it on my nose all casually and stuff, right, and the class burst into laughter. My teacher said if I was going to be such a "class clown," I ought to wear the nose all day long. So I accepted the challenge and put it on.

The best part of it all was watching the expression change on Eleanor's face: first, seeing the clown nose, then second, her realization that it was *me* wearing the clown nose. She broke into this huge fit of giggles and I crossed the line in the middle of the stairs to walk down with her. I accidentally bumped into a ton of kids but it wasn't a big wreck or anything. She gave me a really hard time about it, though. She didn't even want to know why I was wearing the clown nose immediately, she was just appalled that I dared to cross the line.

Then I explained the whole math class thing to her, and she told me how when she was a little girl she actually wanted to be a clown. She said she had these fleece clown onesie pajamas that she wore all the time, and decided that she *was* a clown. Her parents didn't like her having whoopee cushions or horns or anything like that, but her aunt got her a clown kit for Christmas that year and she loved it. She would leave whoopee cushions under the couch pillows and once put on a ton of her mom's lipstick on to look like a clown. And then, as she got older, she got really into juggling. I didn't believe that part. I told her she had to prove it to me but she said she couldn't in a hallway of all places and besides, she had to go to her AP Marine Biology class.

Katie Mlinek

By the end of her story the bell was about to ring, so I had to turn around quick and run to class. I wondered why I was getting so many other strange looks as I rushed to my Physics class, then realized I still had the nose on. I had forgotten in the midst of her story. Later, in English, the second-to-last period of the day, I kept begging her the whole time to *please* just juggle something, just for one *itsy bitsy second*, and she said she wasn't as good anymore but she could try. So we looked around the room and got three wooden rulers from kids and oh my gosh, she juggled them like she had been doing it since birth. It was amazing. Miranda clapped like crazy once Eleanor stopped.

I bowed at her feet and took off my nose.

"You are much more deserving," I said, handing it to her. "I bequeath this clown nose upon you, as a mark of your crazy pencil juggling talents, for you to wear for the rest of the day."

The Eleanor I thought I knew would never take the nose. She would laugh a little and sort of pretend that she didn't notice me holding out the nose to her, or wave it away all polite or something. But I was wrong. Eleanor took the nose. She put it on and gave it a little honk. And if my heart was that big red blob on her nose, it would have squeezed so tight she'd never be able to breathe.

Comic Sans

Chapter 8

Miranda has quickly created a tradition that she calls "The Daily Squeeze" in English. It's basically where she gives everyone a bear hug at the beginning of each class. At first it was funny and all, you know, each of us standing around being squeezed by this teeny girl, but it got tiring *real* fast. She has the same amount of enthusiasm for it every day and I just can't take it, I really can't. Eleanor always gives her a hug back, though. Veronica literally pushed Miranda away by the second day and Mason always goes to the bathroom in the beginning of class so he misses it every time. I think the timing of his bathroom trip is purposeful. At least I don't run away. I take it like a man. Which is to say that I stand there and don't do anything at all and just wait until it's over.

After "The Daily Squeeze," we all gather around the computer, Eleanor normally at the helm, and research whatever is next on the rubric. It would be better if we had more computers, or if any of us at least had a laptop, but none of us do. So we stay crammed around that little desktop screen.

It's wickedly warm in the English room, too. I always get worried that I'll start to sweat too much and stink up our little corner, especially since I have P.E. right before class, so I put extra deodorant on each morning. Today, I put some on, let it dry, then put even more on. It's supposed to be ninety degrees, which really means school should be cancelled but apparently The Suits at the top didn't think so.

The way we were all gathered around the computer today, I was closest to Eleanor. I think I could smell the shampoo from her hair but maybe the heat was just getting to me. We were looking through the military history of Denmark and I was wondering if it would be weird if I asked Eleanor if she used strawberry shampoo and Veronica was texting some guy while smacking gum right in my ear. Mason wasn't back from the bathroom yet.

"Did you guys click on that article I sent?" Veronica asked. "About the parrot that could recite Hamlet's big speech or whatever?"

Immediately, everyone in the group perked up.

"That was better than butternut squash!" Miranda said.

"When I first saw that, I thought 'hot tamales!'" Eleanor said. They all started laughing. I just looked at them.

"What?" I asked.

"You didn't see that?" Eleanor asked. "On the group chat?"

I shook my head. "I lost my phone. Over the weekend."

"Bummer," Veronica said.

"A real 'crame'," Miranda said. Everyone laughed, even Mason who had just come back from the bathroom, and again I was the only one who was clueless about the joke.

Eleanor turned to me. "Another chat joke," she explained. I nodded, but I felt all droopy inside, like a helium balloon that's been left out for too long. Or when you shake a pencil just right and it starts to look like rubber. I'm a rubber pencil. What a thing to be.

Comic Sans

"Hey, we should put something about that line in our presentation," I said, pointing to the computer screen. Anything to change the topic.

"'There is no other country that rhymes with Denmark?'" Eleanor read from the screen. She giggled. "You want to put that in the presentation?"

"Heck yeah," I said, and everyone laughed. It made me feel a little better.

"What about Bismark?" Veronica asked.

"Not a country," Mason said.

"Quadrimark?" Miranda asked. We all paused and looked at each other.

"I don't think that's a country," Mason said hesitantly. Miranda grinned and we all laughed again.

"Someone should ask a parrot to see if it can recite everything that rhymes with Denmark," Veronica said.

"Or how many hot tamales it can eat in thirty seconds," Miranda said. And everyone laughed again, enjoying the sweetness of their newfound bond, while I just sat there. You know, I didn't even feel hot at all anymore. I was feeling more chilly, to tell you the truth. Chilly in early May.

Katie Mlinek

Chapter 9

When I got home, I was super exhausted. I stepped on my foot all weird while walking up our front steps so my ankle was hurting, to make things even better. And when I tried to use the bathroom the stupid toilet wouldn't flush, and then I couldn't find the dill pickle chips *again*, and Dad was passed out on the couch snoring his life away. So I flopped on the chair opposite him and flipped the TV to something else, since I figured he wouldn't mind. It was at least semi-peaceful. But then, when Mom got home a couple of minutes later, it was like she brought a tornado with her.

"Come help me get the stupid groceries out of the trunk," she snapped. Dad woke up with a jolt and rubbed his eyes. "I'm talking to both of you," she said.

"Alright, alright," he groaned, and we went out to get the four bags of groceries from the car. I could have carried them all myself, really. *She* could have carried them all herself. But she had that fire in her eyes that told both Dad and me to not fight back today.

She had already moved on to the next thing to be angry about as we put the groceries away.

Comic Sans

"Who in the world didn't have the brains to flush the toilet properly?" she yelled, stomping into the kitchen. "I don't understand. It's *so simple*. All you have to do is *press a button*."

Dad and I looked at each other. "It's one of you two, and it won't be that tough to figure out who," she said.

"The toilet is messed up or something," I said. "It just won't flush."

She looked at me with a raised eyebrow, suspending her belief, and went back to the bathroom. Dad and I stood frozen in the kitchen as we listened to her try to flush the toilet.

"Great!" she yelled with a sarcastic laugh from the bathroom. "Now we have to call a plumber, too!"

"We have to fix the brakes on the car first, honey, remember?" Dad said softly as she came back into the kitchen. But Mom was like a wild animal. I had hardly seen her so psychotic. The last time she was in this bad a mood was when no one showed up to help her with the bakery sale at the elementary school. It's ridiculous, it really is.

"We'll deal with the car later. We aren't going to die in that thing anytime soon. But I will not live in a house with urine just floating in open bowls."

"We might not have money to deal with the car later," Dad said. I could tell he was starting to get irritated, too. I wanted to leave but Mom was still standing at the entrance, and I'd have to ask her to move to get around her. Who knows what eruption *that* would cause. "I could try to fix the toilet myself. We can work this out," Dad said.

"Yeah, remember the last time you tried to fix something? We didn't have a window for a *month*. We are getting a plumber."

Katie Mlinek

I remember that. One of the neighborhood teenagers thought it would be funny to go around to all the houses and throw rocks at the window, to see if people would go up to them or something. Only their rock *broke* our window. Dad swore he could install a window pane by himself, and ended up dropping the sheet of glass all over the floor. I was younger then, around five or six maybe, and accidentally stepped on one of the pieces of glass and Dad felt really bad and Mom got all mad and didn't talk to him much again until he came back from his next long trip away.

"Honey, we *don't have the money*," Dad said. The tips of his ears were starting to get red. I'd never seen someone look so torn up inside as Dad did now. Mom's angry now, but she'll get over it eventually. Dad, though...this was getting to him deep.

Mom pulled out a giant wad of crisp twenty-dollar bills from her pocket and slapped it on the table. There had to have been five hundred dollars there. Out of nowhere, five hundred dollars, just like that.

"There," she said, "Take it."

Dad and I just looked at it.

"You know where this came from? My earrings. All of them except for my wedding pearls. The lady at the pawn shop was very excited."

Dad deflated a little. It all made sense now. The bad mood, the anger, the stomping around. Those earrings were practically her only prized possessions. And now they were officially out of her polishing routine, forever.

"Honey...."

"I don't want to hear it, David. Someone has to make money around here."

Comic Sans

"You know I've been looking for a job –"

"Right, and I know you definitely weren't sleeping on the couch when I got home."

Even though Mom kept throwing her digs at Dad, I felt terrible. I looked at both of my parents and saw how heavy their eyes were, how bloodshot and wrinkled and droopy they seemed.

"I'll call a plumber," Dad said.

Mom nodded, looked like she was going to say one last thing before deciding against it, and left the kitchen. The twenty-dollar bills stayed on the table.

Chapter 10

I feel like having a school project on *Hamlet* is the most cliché English class thing ever. Somewhere, embedded in the subconscious of students, we know it's going to happen at some point. Just like we know we'll have to finally memorize all the parts of a sentence for some test and know what the heck a gerund is supposed to be. Though 80s high school movies are the most stupid, unrealistic thing ever, there is one thing they get right: school assignments are *boring*. This project is no different. Everyone is basically doing a presentation on the same thing, and then we're all going to have to watch each other spew information we've already known for the past however many weeks.

It's getting towards the end of the year, so Mrs. Desarrollee gave this to us as a "slow, easy, fun project." Why can't we just watch movies, like in every other class? We could *watch* Hamlet, for goodness sake. It would probably take just as long and people would still goof around just as much. If there's one thing I'm glad for, it's my luck in randomly being assigned this group. I've hardly paid attention to most of the kids in this English class, except for the ones who talk constantly because they're *dying* for attention (always using big terms like "synecdoche" or "enjambment"). Other than Eleanor, whose existence I was at least aware of, I hardly knew these kids. But since this whole project thing, I actually kind of look forward to English. Okay. Not true. The only reason I enjoy school at *all* is English class. The rest of school

Comic Sans

is like a swampy pond. I can muddle through it okay, but I feel all gross afterwards.

"We actually have to get some real work done today, guys," Eleanor said as the group gathered together.

Mason groaned.

"How about tomorrow?" Veronica asked, popping a Hubba Bubba bubble. She was sitting with her back to the table and her legs over the chair. "Or Thursday. Or how bout next week?"

"Next week sounds great, but we could work hard now and rest next week," Eleanor said.

"If we all close our eyes right now, and then open them up on the count of three, maybe the presentation will magically appear," Miranda said.

"I hate this," Mason groaned. "This is stupid. Everything sucks. School sucks. Hamlet sucks. What's the big deal with Hamlet, anyways? He's just a whiny baby with mommy issues."

"His *dad* just died!" Miranda said.

"Yeah, so? If your dad dies tomorrow, you're not going to think about killing someone and then think about killing yourself because you didn't kill someone."

"You're depressing," Veronica said.

"Blame Hamlet. He got me all depressed," Mason said.

"I think Silent James over here is the real depressing one," Eleanor said, nudging me.

I just looked at them and smiled. I really didn't want to respond, not because I didn't want to talk to them or anything, but just opening my mouth really hurt. See, you break a bone in your body and you put a cast on it and it's fine, right? But you get one cut, *one little cut* in your mouth, and that's it for a week. All you can ever think about is how painful it is. Every time you have to talk or eat or even sigh, you feel it like a bullet hole in your cheek. And you can't say, "Oh, sorry I'm talking all weird, I have an *open wound inside of me*." You just have to suck it up and wait for it to go away. But then it never does! It never does. Gah. It stinks. Once it's finally gone you feel like a veteran, a brave soldier coming back from the ashes of war, but to everyone else it's just another Tuesday.

When I woke up this morning, I felt it. Now I'm going to wake up every morning hoping it's gone but it never will be. What if I still have it during the interview? But I don't want to think about that. I don't want to worry about that now.

"Yeah, James, what's with the silent treatment?" Veronica asked. She took her legs off the back of the chair and whirled around.

I shrugged. "It hurts to talk," I said.

"Oh my God, what happened?" Veronica snapped into a serious mode I hadn't seen in her before. I don't know if she swallowed her gum or something, but she seemed really, legitimately concerned and alert all of a sudden. I looked around at the rest of the group and they were, too. Eleanor was watching me carefully and biting her bottom lip.

"Oh my gosh, guys, not like *that*," I said. "I just have a sore in my mouth. Right in the corner of my cheek. Every time I talk, my teeth scrape up against it and it hurts."

Mason was the first to laugh. Really, he guffawed, which Eleanor pointed out to me later as being his "laughing style." Veronica ended up laughing so hard she *snorted*.

"Those are the worst," Eleanor said. "I hate it when they're on the inside of your lip and they rest up right against your front teeth."

Comic Sans

"Dude, yes!" Veronica said, still laughing. "You made it seem like someone *died*, James!"

"That's what I thought," Mason said. "I thought this was about to be the most awkward class ever."

"What do you call those things? Sores inside your mouth?" Miranda asked.

"We call them canker sores, but I don't know what they're really called," Eleanor said. "I can figure it out and send it to the group chat."

"But then I won't know!" I said.

"Oh, that's right," Eleanor said. "I forgot. And sorry you had to say that out loud, that looked like it hurt. Here. You can write everything down on this notepad for the rest of class." She gave me a whole notepad of paper and everyone giggled.

"THANKS" I wrote in all caps on the first page with a little smiley face right underneath it. Everyone laughed again.

"Looks like we're not going to get any work done still," I wrote, and pushed it towards Eleanor. She laughed and turned to the computer.

"Alrighty," she said, cracking her knuckles. "Let's get something done, guys. For real, now."

Mason groaned again, Veronica flipped her legs back around, and Miranda scooted in her chair. I kept the notepad next to me, close.

Katie Mlinek

Chapter 11

Dad called Len the Plumber, but the guy who showed up was named Rick, not Len, so I was pretty disappointed. Everything around the house felt weird, like sawdust, all flimsy and unstable. All three of us were tiptoeing around everything. Saying, "can you please pass the milk," suddenly had to be carefully calculated and worded. I biked more just to get out of the house. Getting a job seemed even more appealing than before, just as a distraction and to have somewhere to go, something to do. To have people to talk to other than my parents.

When I biked, it was aimlessly. Though the other day I biked past Beard-O's house because I noticed that his mailbox disappeared and I was really curious if it would just reappear again at some point. And I always liked to bike past the one fancy house with the koi pond because they have to get new fish all the time, like they can't take care of them properly or something. I saw "Ben" out on Elmswood Road a lot, which I liked to bike on since cars hardly drive there, though I always see old, flabby shirtless guys mowing their lawn and it's gross. But I always felt way too awkward to go near Eleanor's house.

Before, I had been slightly nervous for the Dollar Tree and Food Lion interviews coming up, but now I felt ready for it. I kind of wanted to get them over with, to tell you the truth. Dad offered to be the one to drive me. I think he just wants to get out of the house some, too.

Comic Sans

On Wednesday, Dad pulled up in front of Food Lion and turned off the engine, looking at me with an encouraging smile that seemed to say, "my son is growing up."

"This is a fire lane, Dad," I said.

"It doesn't matter. You can just hop out here," he said.

"It'd be nice to start a job by getting in trouble for parking illegally."

Dad turned the engine back on. "There. Better?"

"Now we're stalling illegally."

He sighed then grinned, as if he could transfer his forced optimism to me. "You're gonna do great. Don't be nervous."

"I'm not nervous." And I really wasn't. If this didn't pan out, I still had two other options. And somewhere, between the three of these, I *had* to get a job.

I practiced a firm handshake with Dad that probably made him feel like a proper father, and went into Food Lion. He didn't pull away until he watched me walk inside. I was perfectly capable of walking in without being watched.

When I got in, though, I realized that I didn't know where to go. I knew the manager's voice from the phone, but not what he looked like or anything. I stood at the entrance of the store for a moment until I realized that an old lady was trying to get around me, so I went over to the customer service desk.

"Hello," I said, putting on my best smile. "I'm here for an interview with the manager? I don't –"

Katie Mlinek

"You must be James, yes?" I turned around and saw a man with a silver nametag. "My name is Mr. Jones. You can follow me to my office."

The manager had a bald circle right on the crown of his head. If I got to get a closer look (which I wouldn't really want, anyways), I would bet that the hair he did have was made up of more dandruff than actual hair. He had an absent sort of smile, like he had spent so many years wearing it that he forgot it was there. I guess as a manager your only job is to smile. Sounds tiring.

He gestured for me to sit down so I did. The manager immediately began to drone on about a level of excellence or something like that and I tried to focus, I really did, but his voice was like a buzzing fly. At first it really bugs you but then you stop noticing it.

"Your resume looks good," the manager said.

I realized that I was absently gazing at the photo on his desk of his younger self and snapped back to the current, balding him. "Oh, thank you," I said. He looked it over more and I bit my lip, hoping he wasn't upset about something.

"So tell me about your experience with the PTMA Foundation for Raising Children," he said.

Shoot. That, yes, I remember writing that. It was really just my elementary school's PTA, which I helped out once by bringing in cookies for a bake sale. Back then I automatically signed Mom up for everything because she was always itching to do something. Writing that down on a resume seemed lame, and I always thought the PTA should be called the Parent Teacher Mutual Alliance, and who doesn't love helping out children? I didn't think these managers would get into the details.

"Well...it's interesting that you bring that up. I had just been planning on going back," I said.

Comic Sans

"Really? What prompted you to return?"

"Oh, you know." I gave him my best manager-worthy smile. "I guess the good feeling I get from helping people out."

"That's a great quality to have. I'm starting to think you were meant to be a cashier," he said.

Managers must not be used to giving out compliments if that's the best he can do. If anything, I was insulted, but I mainly just didn't know how to feel. I smiled and nodded, figuring it was neutral enough for him to interpret it however he wanted.

"So I can certainly give you my ideas of who you are right now, after seeing you here and looking over your resume. But first, I'd like to know how you'd describe yourself," he said.

Oh, geez. This is an interview to be a *cashier*, and stores don't pay cashiers to be interesting people. I really want to like this guy, and this job, but I just…can't. I just want minimum wage, you know? No personal involvement, or soul-searching questions, just a nametag and a timecard and a starchy uniform.

"Mr. Watterworth?" the manager said.

I had been looking at his photo again. "I would say that I'm very…personable. I'm willing to talk to anyone." Not true. But you have to give these people what they want.

The manager leaned back. I think some of his joints creaked. "I'll tell you what I think of you, Mr. Watterworth. I think you're a very nice man. But we expect more than nice here. We need above and beyond customer service, constant attention to the consumer, and positive energy. Do you think you can be that sort of employee?"

"Excuse me, sorry?"

He breathed out long and low. I didn't mean for that to sound rude in any way, he just said a lot of words at once, but when he didn't respond for an uncomfortably long time, I immediately became worried that it might have come across that way. Even though I have two other places where I can interview, getting this job feels really important all of a sudden. I'd even be willing to pay for my own uniform.

"I mean, yes. Yes…sir," I stumbled. My brain was whirring too much.

"Well, I know I certainly have a lot to mull over. It was a pleasure to meet you, James. I'll be in touch."

"Thank you," I said.

We shook hands again and he walked me to the door of his office. I didn't look back, but I heard the door shut behind me with an audible thud.

I had to walk through the entire store to get to the front sliding doors. It was terrible. I felt like I had botched it right at the end. I don't even know what happened. Maybe I just started caring *too* much, and my brain turned to squash. But it's not squash season, you know? It's almost summer. I should be more alive now than ever, but I feel like a dust bunny, all raggedy and unwanted and stuffed in unimportant places and hating it all the while.

Comic Sans

Chapter 12

I had to walk across the entire lot to get to Dad's car, which was parked in the very back.

"How'd it go?" he asked as I opened up the door.

"Why are you parked in the back?" I climbed in.

He scanned my face. "It went badly?"

"Yeah." For some reason, I really didn't feel like talking. I just felt tired. Like an old tire that's been rolling for too long.

"What happened?" he asked.

"Our personalities just didn't mesh, I guess." More like I lost my cool. Got distracted super easily. Not sure how Dad would respond to something like that.

"I'm sure the Dollar Tree will be different."

"Maybe."

"Do you think there's a chance of you getting the job, still?"

"No. Probably not."

Dad gripped the wheel and looked like he was trying to hold back a sigh. "It'll be different at the Dollar Tree."

I noticed all of the little whiskers starting to come in on his face. His forehead was heavy with wrinkles and his eyes seemed to droop. Suddenly I felt bad about the whole thing. I feel like I'm weighing Dad and Mom down. Maybe I'm part of why they've been fighting and stuff. I just suck up resources and don't do anything. We pulled into the shopping center with a Dollar Tree tucked in the corner.

"You're right," I said, getting out. "This one will be different."

He gave me two thumbs up but didn't wait to watch me walk in.

The first thing I noticed in this particular Dollar Tree was the whole rack of Ring Pops set almost directly in front of the door. They were neon and only 55 cents. I thought I could get one for Eleanor – as a joke, of course – but I only had two quarters in my pocket. I could ask Dad for a nickel out in the car, but then he'd ask questions and I'd probably feel too tired to explain. It was a shame, really. They were the probably the only things in the store that were actually under a dollar.

The whole thing smelled like plastic, just like Eleanor said. I thought of the rug in that first grade classroom and Brett and how he always stole my spot. But I shook the memory away as quickly as it came and started looking for the manager's door. I walked past it three times, each time thinking it was a bathroom or stock room or something, before noticing the tiny plastic plaque that said "Mr. Rooney" on it. I knocked and a voice wheezed, "Come in."

There was another plaque on a fold-up table (I think it was supposed to be a desk) that said "Mr. Rooney." The desk was crowded with unlabeled manila folders, eye drops, and crumpled

Comic Sans

tissues. A weasel of a man behind the table was wearing an untucked button-up shirt.

"Yes?" he asked. He sniffed and I noticed that his nose was red.

"Hi, I'm James Watterworth, I'm here for an interview?" I don't know why I said it like a question. The blank look on the man's face made me start thinking everything in questions. Not like Jeopardy, but like my sanity was in jeopardy. See, I was already becoming kitschy. The room was a vortex of everything that was off-white and unclean. Not that it was *dirty*, I don't really have an eye for cleanliness, but just standing there made me feel gross.

Mr. Rooney gestured for me to have a seat in the collapsible metal chair in the corner of the room. I noticed faint music playing, but I couldn't tell whether it was from his Dona XP laptop or the store. The music sounded like it was dying, dipping suddenly between pitches and sometimes coming to a complete stop.

He sniffed gruffly while typing on his computer. I started to wonder if, in his sniffling fit, he had already forgotten all about me. At one point he was only hitting the backspace button. Finally he shut his laptop and turned to face me.

"Hello, mister, uh –"

"Watterworth," I quickly said, holding out a hand. "James Watterworth."

"Mr. Watterworth." He looked down at my hand with a brief look of disgust before giving it a limp shake. Then he laced his bony fingers together and looked at me. We sat in silence like that for a few minutes, me looking around the walls for anything to focus on but him, Mr. Rooney staring at me. Actually, I can't really know if he was looking at me or not since I wasn't looking

Katie Mlinek

at him, but I just had a feeling. That gross feeling of being watched.

"So, mister, uh...young man," he finally said. "What complaints do you have about The Dollar Tree?"

"Actually, I'm here for that interview," I said, fidgeting a little.

This man was starting to make me mad, what with his red nose and two name plaques and the like. But I had to keep it under control. After all, Dad was waiting for good news and I was waiting for this interview to be over.

"Oh, yes, that...yes. You told me. Do you have a resume?" he asked. He wiped his nose with a tissue.

I took it out without responding and handed it over. He barely ran his eyes over it.

"Very nice, very professional," he said.

Now I was getting mad. This guy was barely even paying attention to this interview. Did he want to hire someone or no? Because I sure as heck want to get hired. But why aren't there any good places out there? Why can't I have my phone so I can be a real part of my English group, or a job to keep me distracted from everything, or just know where the chips are in my own house?

"Why do you want to work here, James?" he asked.

If I told him everything, he'd be soaked in angst by the end of it. So I kept it simple. "Well, I like talking to people and I've been going to the Dollar Tree as long as I can remember. I guess you can say it's a nostalgia thing."

You know, to make this worse, I have to lie about myself the whole time. Because on my own, I'm really not good enough. Why is the truth always the worst thing to say during these types of things?

Comic Sans

Mr. Rooney nodded slowly, closing his eyes as if he was meditating on my words. Suddenly, he opened his eyes again and spewed out a giant, honking, wet sneeze. I could see little snot splatters on his desk. I'm telling you, it was one of the grossest things I've ever witnessed and I even had to change my cousin's diaper once when she was little. There are few things worse than that. They live on the other side of the country now and she's probably like ten years old and doesn't wear diapers anymore. But here I go again, getting distracted by nothing.

"I'm sorry that you're so sick," I said. "Do you want to reschedule the interview?"

"No," he said. "No, I think we're finished here. I'll give you a call next week."

"Okay," I said, a little unsure. It all felt so quick. But I got up to leave. "It was nice to meet you."

"Likewise," he said.

It was only after I left his office that I really registered what he had said. *A call next week.* Would he even remember that any of this happened, though?

As I walked out to the car, that's when I remembered – I don't even have a cell phone. Why didn't I think about this sort of thing? It's so basic – give someone your phone number so they can actually call you. How is he going to call me? I don't think he has our house phone number. I thought about turning around and going back inside, but would that really help anything? He'd probably write it down on one of his snot-coated tissues and lose it in the trash bin. And Dad could already see me walking towards the car, and I'd feel all self-conscious if I turned around and ran back inside. So I just kept walking. There was nothing to do but that.

Katie Mlinek

Chapter 13

We have two cafeterias that we're assigned, one called Big Cafeteria and the other called Junior Cafeteria, because kids in my school can't be more creative than that. You better hope you're assigned to the Big Caf with any friend at all or else say goodbye to fun lunch times. I've been assigned to the Junior Caf three years in a row. It's terrible. All the kids who have in-school suspension have to eat lunch in there, too, at a special table in the corner, and there's always someone there. The only thing I look forward to is seeing who it is for the week. This one kid (who calls himself JT but is really named Frederick) is there the most. He always puts a napkin in his lap while he eats. It's really strange. You'd think a kid with such good table manners would behave, too. At least his mother taught him *something*. But other than getting to see juvenile delinquents' eating habits, all of lunch sucks.

But today I didn't have to sit in the Junior Cafeteria. It was an HSA day, which means a bunch of freshmen would be taking that test you have to pass in order to graduate high school, and they'd be taking it in our English classroom. Which means I get a different lunch time, and a different classroom, and it's not even a real class. It's just a study hall period.

School is really stupid. I mean, we have to take all these tests that don't matter to anyone except teachers to see if they're teaching right. And the thing is, they spend all year teaching us how to take the tests. So really the tests are testing how well the

Comic Sans

teachers can teach the test. I'm getting dizzy just saying that. It makes no sense, is what I'm trying to get at.

And the other thing about tests is that it messes up all the schedules. I wore my biggest, coziest T-shirt today so that when I have to go to study hall, I can take a nap. And I brought extra pencils in case I can't fall asleep and want to build a pencil castle or something instead. Teachers always say to come to class prepared and they can't say I'm not prepared.

Anyways, I walked into the Big Cafeteria and went over to a table in the corner, one that seats four people near the triangle windows. What kind of place has triangle windows? My stupid school, that's what. But as I started walking over there, I saw one person run up to it and take a seat. Normally I'm sort of by myself during lunch, but I figured I could at least still ask to sit there and pretend to do homework in awkward silence or something. But then three more kids pulled chairs from other tables and gathered around the first kid. Ah. So they were an exclusive group. I hate that stuff. Cemented groups of people. How do you join a group? Are there rules? Are you required to wear contact lenses that change your eye color, or have brass chains sticking out of your pocket, or have a homemade second ear piercing that's always infected? Because that's how people seem to categorize themselves in high school.

I looked around the cafeteria, figuring I could sit with the computer nerds that always stay so close together they actually start to look like a circuit board, but I didn't see them. Finally, I noticed Eleanor sitting with Miranda at a table nearby and walked over there.

"Mind if I join you ladies?" I asked. I don't think I sounded too desperate, which was sort of how I was feeling, if you want to know the truth.

"Sure," Eleanor said.

Katie Mlinek

I slid into the seat beside her and opened up my lunchbox. Mom still always made my lunch. She had been for all my life. When I was in middle school, I took out the nice little recyclable containers she put everything in and replaced them with normal sandwich bags, so people wouldn't realize my mom was making my lunch. She used to write me notes every day, sometimes with quotes, sometimes with just an "I ♥ U! XOXO MOM" but finally stopped when I got to high school. It took her that long to think I was too old for that kind of stuff. I always threw them away on the bus in the morning before anyone could notice.

Miranda obviously made her lunch herself. It was a bag of Doritos, princess gummies, a bottle of Gatorade, and a Little Debbie brownie. She opened up the bottle of Gatorade and chugged it all in one go. I could see her gulps go down her throat, her esophagus clearly straining to move so much liquid to her stomach in such little time. It happened so fast, I didn't even think to start chanting "chug, chug, chug!" until the bottle was already empty.

"Woah," Eleanor said, "That was weirdly very impressive."

Miranda shrugged, wiped her mouth, and started staring out of the triangle window. We all sat in silence.

"So, uh…what are you guys going to do during our study hall period?" I asked. Anything to break the ice. I don't know why I felt so weird and awkward.

"App-sigh," Eleanor said.

"What?"

"You know. Like AP Psychology. AP Psy."

"Oh." Now I felt all awkward and embarrassed for not knowing something like that. It's a whole other world, all the AP this and Honors that. It's a load of crap, if you ask me. AP English is the only AP class I've taken or probably ever will take. I

Comic Sans

don't even know what good it will do me. I hate all the kids who only take AP classes and think they're way smarter than everyone else, just because they're better at plagiarizing answers or something. Eleanor isn't like that, though. She really is smart, and she doesn't rub it in anyone's face ever or anything. She just knows the answer to anything if you ask her. She's like Google.

"My cousin said that class always made her cry," Miranda said.

"Really? That's strange. It's not *that* bad. English is worse, I think," Eleanor said.

"Does English make you cry?" I asked, sensing the opportunity for a good tease.

"No. Only you make me cry," Eleanor said, trying to hide her grin. Dang. She got to me before I could get to her.

"Well, you might as well stab me with that spork. There's no point in living anymore. I would never want to make you mad or cry or anything. I mean, if I ever make you cry, you can punch me in the face. I won't mind. I'll deserve it. You can punch me in the face right now, if you want."

Eleanor giggled. "I don't think you could ever *really* make me cry," she said. "And I'm never going to punch you in the face, you silly. Besides, I never cry. I'm more of a screamer, believe it or not. Truly. So you don't have to worry about it." She nudged my elbow and my stomach got all jittery.

"What do you mean you never cry? Everybody cries *some* time," I said. "Break an arm while mowing, Christmas tree falls on you, zombie eats your foot off. There are plenty of reasons to cry."

She laughed. "The last time I remember crying was when I had a nosebleed for the first time. My nose bleeds all the time now, though," Eleanor said.

Katie Mlinek

"Really? Why did that make you cry, though?" I asked.

"I thought it was my brain coming out of my nose. My parents thought I was just being silly but they ended up having to take me to the doctor to convince me otherwise."

"Oh my gosh! How old were you? And how often does your nose bleed?"

"I was pretty little. I remember it was around my clown phase, because I had to wash my clown costume since it got blood over it. My nose still bleeds sometimes. Mostly in winter, though."

"That's crazy," I said. "I mean, really! Why haven't you used this to get out of gym class before? I bet you anything you could do it."

Eleanor shrugged. "I'd rather get physically beat up than let people think I've got weird problems."

"Yeah, someone would assume you have a stomach worm or a permanent period or something strange like that," Miranda said.

Alright. That's my cue to stop talking. If there was ever a dangerous territory for man, it's when girls casually mention menstrual cycles in conversations.

"Yeah...kickball is better than that," Eleanor said.

"Well, my first thought would be that you had abnormally dry nostrils," I said, trying to recover from all the awkwardness Miranda just created. Play it off cool, you know. "That's what I always assume when people ask to go to the nurse in the middle of class."

Eleanor laughed. "Did you know that there's a Nosebleed font?"

"What?"

Comic Sans

"Yeah, really! It's all drippy and stuff, like a real nose bleed."

"Why couldn't they call it Runny Boogers or something?" Miranda asked. "It sounds like it looks like plain old runny boogers."

"This is officially the worst conversation for lunch ever," I said, laughing.

Eleanor shrugged. "Good question. I don't know. That would probably be a more inclusive name, though. Everyone deals with runny noses."

"Or Nose Picker," Miranda said.

"What?"

"That could be another name. Nose Picker. Everyone picks their noses a little bit."

I was losing it. "Holy crap, Miranda!" My stomach was starting to hurt from laughing so hard.

"It's true! When it gets a little crusty right at the bottom and no one is around, you just use your finger to flake it off. Everyone does it. But no one talks about it."

Eleanor and I looked at each other with wide eyes, cracking up. "You're right…and there's probably a font for that," Eleanor said.

Just then the lunch bell rang, and I waited for Eleanor to gather up her stuff so I could walk out of lunch beside her. Miranda ran her fingers along the lockers and walked like a tightrope walker on the right side of the hallway. She quickly fell behind us as the post-lunch crowd surged ahead. She was a weird girl, but I really got a kick out of her. She was probably more unique than anyone here.

Katie Mlinek

Eleanor glanced back over her shoulder at Miranda as if she was thinking the same thing as me. "You know, Miranda and I used to take ballet lessons together," she said. "Back when we were three or so."

"Really?" I said. "I can't imagine her in a pink tutu. Or you."

"Yeah, really. There's a picture of us where her hair got stuck in my tutu somehow and we had to cut a huge chunk of her hair off to get it out. In the picture, I'm screaming like I'm being tortured but she looks perfectly happy just sitting on the floor with her hair being tugged."

"Yikes. Did your nose start bleeding from all the stress?"

"Oh, it never stopped." She smiled and stopped walking. "Hey, stupid, the study hall room is right here."

She called me stupid. This is the happiest I've ever been being called stupid.

Comic Sans

Chapter 14

Mason is the sort of guy who, once he realizes he's losing, will change the rules of the game to give himself a shot at a comeback. Well actually, that's just a hunch I have. We have P.E. together right before English, and we do stupid games in that class all the time, and his face gets really red when he loses or messes up or something. He mentioned once that he has two older brothers, and I bet he melted down during their games all the time. There was this kid on my street who used to do that when we were all younger and played soccer together. I used to love doing stuff like that. Playing games like soccer. But P.E. is just pure torture.

If anyone ever said they enjoyed P.E., they were lying. The humid locker rooms, the grimy gym, the lunging and crunching and heart-pumping. It's all horrible. We have to sit in these rows called "squads," and I sit across from Mason in the next squad. I don't really know too many other people in the class, but you don't really have to when you spend most of the time stretching your arms and legs in each other's faces.

I was already sitting in my squad group when Mason came and sat down. I could see the sweat stains on his gym shirt that had been there all year. I don't think he's taken them home to wash them even once. At least it smells like that.

"Alright everyone, today we're going to take those yoga positions we've been practicing and advance to some more complicated positions," my teacher, Mr. Wasserman, said. "For these moves you'll need a partner, so choose someone you're comfortable with."

Mason turned and looked at me. I nodded. Guess that makes us partners now. Everyone got up and grabbed the yoga mats we've had to use the past couple of classes now. I hate this unit. I'm really not flexible, and Mr. Wasserman plays this horrible YouTube playlist of royalty-free, relaxing piano music. The girl's gym class this period has been doing nothing but push-ups this unit, and even that's better than this yoga crap. But man, I'm glad there aren't girls in this class. That would be *weird*.

Mason and I kicked our shoes off to the side and sat down on the mat. Someone had scratched a number and, in bubbly writing, "call me" on the foam mat. Mason looked at it and scratched the phone number out. Above it, using his fingernail, he wrote, "877-359-STAR." I started cracking up. It's from this commercial that everyone knows, where a girl keeps trying to be good at things like dancing and piano and singing but every time she tries, she falls on her face. So she calls 877-359-STAR and gets a professional trainer or something. It's so stupid, how much she fell on her face. Even while sitting down to play piano. And then at the end, it's a big deal because she can sing the phone number really well after getting some lessons. I stinkin' love that commercial.

"You remember that?" Mason asked.

"Yeah! 'If you want to go somewhere far, call 877-359-STAR,'" I sang.

"Yes! I loved that commercial when I was little," Mason said.

"Does anyone not have a partner?" Mr. Wasserman asked. "Someone should be left over. We don't have an even number today since Michael is absent." Some kid raised his hand. I don't think I had even noticed him in my class before. "Austin, come

Comic Sans

over here and demonstrate these yoga positions with me for the class."

Mason snorted under his breath. "Sucks for that guy," he said. I just nodded.

Mr. Wasserman made us do some stretches, put on the puke-inducing piano music, then went straight into the yoga. There was no easing into it from here. The first one was called the "double down dog." It was where one person keeps their hands and feet on the ground and lifts their rear end up in a v-shape. The other person has to keep their hands on the ground, but prop their feet up in a ninety degree angle against the other person's lower back. Basically, pushing your feet against their butt.

"This is really awkward," I said.

"Well, at least you're not Austin having to do this with Mr. Wasserman," Mason said.

I laughed. "You're right. I feel more grateful now. Thanks."

I looked over at Mr. Wasserman and that kid, blood rushing to my face bent towards the ground, and laughed so hard again I collapsed against the mat. Mason thudded against the mat and I rolled over to look at him. His face was bright red, the same bright red as when he missed a goal during our lacrosse unit, and my heart dropped to my stomach. I was expecting a fireball to shoot out of his head or steam to start spewing out of his ears. But instead he pulled himself up into a sitting position and wiped his hands off.

"So, new rule," he said. "If we fall while trying to hold one of these stupid moves, we don't have to try again."

I nodded and smiled, mostly just relieved he wasn't super angry.

Katie Mlinek

"And another thing," Mason said, "we don't have to try *that hard* in the first place."

I just looked at him.

"Do you catch my drift?" he asked.

I shrugged. "I've never really tried that hard in this class anyways," I said.

"What I mean is that the chance of me messing up almost immediately is very, *very* high. You see?"

I laughed. "Oh! Okay. I see," I said, giving my cheesiest wink.

For the rest of class, Mason and I would start to try the yoga pose and purposefully fail before we had even accomplished it. We were working like real partners, each sensing when the other was ready to give up. Then we would just lie back on the yoga mat while the rest of the class and Mr. Wasserman tried their best. In a strange way, Mason was starting to feel like a real person. Not that he hadn't been real before, but I didn't realize how little I knew him. It's weird how that can happen. How you can be in classes and groups with people and still never really know them. And I had the feeling I was only just beginning to know Mason.

Comic Sans

Chapter 15

Mom and Dad just banned the A/C.

Okay. Maybe I worded that a little harshly. They certainly didn't word it that way. It wasn't as carefully announced this time as the phone or dishwasher, and now that I think about it, they haven't even said anything official about the fact that we're now getting Wonder Bread and haven't had as much as apples in the house for a month.

Needless to say, I was furious. I mean, I didn't tell Mom or Dad that I was or anything, but I also didn't tell them I was going to ride my bike, so they probably could have seen that I was pretty angry.

The A/C. Really? Just as we're about to hit the beginning of the summer heat wave and I already sweat enough as it is. Now home is just as bad as school. Everything Mom and Dad have taken away was more important to me than them. My phone mattered more to me than them. They never used their cell phones. I was the one who always had to load the dishwasher, which wasn't a bad chore, but now I'm the one who ends up getting the worst hits (even though we're supposed to rotate night to night). And now I'm the one who can't stand feeling sweaty, and I can't have any A/C to ever feel cooled down. Do I not matter enough to Mom and Dad?

I was so angry that as I biked, I didn't even pay attention to where I was going. And I didn't pay attention to the fact that I was heading straight towards Eleanor's house, or that from a distance I could see a fuzzy body lying on the grass right outside it, or how that fuzzy body waved to me, and how, as it came closer into my sight range, I was looking straight into the face of Eleanor Iding.

I stopped the bike and tried my best not to pant.

"Goodness, you don't look too comfortable," Eleanor said. She was lying with her back up against the bird bath and had a sketchbook in front of her. She was surrounded by funny-looking markers.

"Yeah, turns out there's no A/C outside," I said, mustering a laugh. Eleanor laughed right back. "What are you up to?" I asked.

"Oh, just doodling," she said, covering up the pages. I wanted to get a closer look but for some reason it really didn't feel right to just leave my bike on the ground and cross the dangerous boundary between the sidewalk and her yard.

"From here it looks like some pretty brilliant stuff," I said, pretending like I was shouting on top of a mountain or something.

She laughed and got up to walk over to me.

"Yeah, sorry. Any people looking out the windows right now must have thought you were talking to a birdbath."

I laughed. "So, what's in the sketchbook?"

She hesitated for a moment, but then showed me. "My parents say you can't do anything with just illustrations and stuff like that, but I still like doing it," she said. "As a hobby, you know."

Comic Sans

On the page was the names of everyone in our English class group written in a different font. Eleanor went through and explained the font and what it meant about each person, how it related to their personality and everything. Mason's looked just like the one Eleanor had described back during the neighborhood block party. Miranda's was light and airy and curly, like vines. Veronica's looked like those stenciled labels on army supply crates.

I waited for Eleanor to say something else, to get to what *my* font was, but she never did. I wasn't even on the page. I felt stupid and selfish and all, for just wanting to hear what my font was. I just had this feeling that she would get it just right, you know? But maybe I just don't have one. Is there a font plain enough to describe plain, normal me? Me with the half-faked resume? Me with nothing to ever do except sweat, ride my bike, and take showers? Me, standing here with this amazing girl on Red Mile Road, knowing I'll never quite be good enough for anything?

Katie Mlinek

Chapter 16

We were eating something Mom had made out of a Crockpot – I swear, I had no idea what it even was, some sort of soup or something – and things were kinda boring, which was at least comforting. Dad was slurping it off his spoon so loud you could have worn earmuffs and it would still sound like he was slurping it right next to your freakin' ear. Mom didn't even notice. I swear, longtime couples just go blind in little ways. Like, they don't notice annoying things about each other anymore. If they did, they probably wouldn't still be married. Mom would go crazy every time Dad slurped his food like the trucker he is and Dad would probably lose his mind whenever she screamed into the phone. She does that. She yells and gets all high pitched like you see people doing in black-and-white movies on those rusty old can-phones.

But anyways, we were pretty quiet at the dinner table. Until Mom had to go and start talking.

"Guess where I was this afternoon," she said. Dad and I looked at each other across the table then back at her, neither of us sure who she was asking or what the answer was.

"*Guess*," she said again.

Dad shrugged. "The grocery store? We need more toilet paper."

Comic Sans

"No, I didn't go to the grocery store. But I'll go tomorrow. Come on now, guess where I was." She looked over at me. "Give it a try, James."

"Redwood?" I asked. That was my old elementary school. I knew there was one day a week that she always had to go there for her PTA meetings but I could never remember which day. Right as I said it, though, I realized I was wrong. Whenever she has to go to those meetings, she comes back fuming and rants all dinner long about the other ladies there. Apparently it's all clique-y and they hate each other's guts. She likes the drama, though, I know it.

"Did you stop by Butterflake?" Dad asked. It's this little bakery in town that doesn't get much business but Mom's a *huge* fan of theirs. She says their cakes are the most delicious, moist things she's ever had in her life. Mom loves baking. She doesn't do it much anymore, and I suspect it's because she's just too tired or maybe the ingredients are too expensive, but I can tell she misses it. She loves to turn on our radio to old jazz or classic rock and spend hours mixing together crazy recipes, spreading bowls and measuring cups out all over the counters just to clean it up again. She says baking is good for everything. It's good for thinking, talking, decision-making, and of course, delicious food. She says it brings people together quicker than anything. And I don't think she's wrong. I mean, if I know someone's offering homemade cupcakes anywhere, I'll be there in two seconds flat.

"No. Fine, I'll just tell you. I went to see a matinee performance at The Scruta!" She looked at us triumphantly.

"The theater?" I asked.

"What play did you see, honey?" Dad asked.

"It was *Taming of the Shrew*," she said.

Katie Mlinek

I snorted. There was something about her seeing *Taming of the Shrew* that felt ironic. Mom turned towards me and suddenly I was worried that she was mad about me snorting. Sometimes – I know this is stupid – but sometimes it feels like she knows what I'm thinking.

"How much are tickets these days?" Dad asked, looking up at her from his bowl.

"It was Pay What You Want Day, actually," Mom said. "So don't worry."

"I wasn't worried," Dad said.

There was nothing but the sound of clinking spoons for a second until Mom turned to me.

"Guess who I saw there?" she asked. She seemed like she was getting really excited now. I was just glad she wasn't mad. I had been bracing myself for another explosion.

"Who?"

"Some friends of yours from school. Guess!"

"We already did a guessing game, honey," Dad said.

"Yeah, well maybe I want to have a little fun, David. I'll tell you one of them." She took a dramatic pause. "Mason Maliosus! He works there!"

"He's not really my friend, Mom," I said. I started to pretend like I was really interested in eating more soup.

"I met another friend of yours, a girl named Eleanor. You haven't told me about her but she said she knew you," Mom said. "She has a very nice family."

"Yeah. She's in my English group." I could feel warmth start to creep into my face. For some reason, I really didn't want Mom to pester me about her.

Comic Sans

"She was a very pretty girl," Mom said. Why was my stupid face getting so stupid red?

"Yeah, she's nice. Can I get more soup or whatever?" I asked.

"Sure, sweetie."

I hate it when Mom calls me a sweetie. I don't even know why, it just makes me feel squirmy. It's like when old ladies tell you that you're "such a dear." I'm not some little Puritan boy or anything, you know?

"Tell your mom about the Dollar Tree interview, James," Dad said.

"Yeah, why don't you ever tell me anything anymore?" Mom asked.

I filled my bowl with more soup than I would eat and came back to the table. "He, I mean, the manager, said he would call me next week to see when I can start," I said.

"Oh, James, that's so exciting!" Mom said.

"Actually, I really want to work at Smith's Gastro Pub," I said. "More money and all. I'd probably like it more, too."

"Oh, okay. Are you sure? You know, places like Food Lion and The Dollar Tree are better for teenagers," Mom said. "They're less demanding, they can work around your school schedule better. Restaurants can be sort of intense. Normally older people work at a place like Smith's. People my age. Or your father's." She gave Dad a pointed look, but he didn't make eye contact with her.

"I just think I'd be pretty, I don't know, unhappy. At a chain store. Just, annoyed and all."

Katie Mlinek

"Well, you're going to do great wherever you end up," she said, touching my shoulder lovingly and all. Everything she was saying felt forced and unnatural.

"Want me to do the dishes? I'll do the dishes," I said. I was really desperate for this conversation to end. Normally we rotate, one of us doing the dishes each night. Even though this wasn't supposed to be my night, I didn't mind staying in the kitchen to wash the dishes that much. I had barely eaten any more of my second bowl of soup but Mom and Dad didn't seem to notice.

"Yes, please," Dad answered for Mom. He slid his bowl towards me and got up from the table.

"Put the rest of the soup in the glass bowl I left on the counter," Mom said.

"Hey, what's for dinner tomorrow?" Dad asked. Mom spun on him.

"What's for dinner tomorrow? What? Dinner today wasn't good enough? You already need dinner for tomorrow?"

Dad held his hands up in surrender. "Woah, I was just curious. That's all. I can help you out with it tomorrow if you need."

"How about you *make* it tomorrow. It'll be the only thing you do all day," Mom said. She spun back around and stormed out of the kitchen. Dad raised his eyebrows at me and followed after her.

For once, I was happy to be cleaning.

Comic Sans

Chapter 17

It was mid-May, and our school was poor as crap, so I was sweating like an Olympic athlete. They can't even afford those cheap little desktop sized fans that keep an area about the size of a hula hoop cold. I once heard that a kid's blood boiled so much that his skin turned red like a lobster and they had to send him home, but it's just a rumor and almost all rumors are bullcrap. It's not really a boiling kind of heat, anyways. Everything is stale, like chips when they get stuck in the back of the closet and you forget they were even there. All I want is a hula hoop spot of fresh air.

It made me think about how sometimes in the summer when you go swimming, you can randomly come across a little cold spot. It never makes sense why there's little areas that are colder or warmer than others in pools, and whenever it's hot as hell outside, those cold spots feel really, really nice. This kid named Justin Gibbey used to live next door to me and his family had one of those above-ground pools that look like crap but are nice when it's the middle of July. He and I used to swim a lot and whenever I found a nice, cold spot I would lie on my back and just sort of soak it all up. But then they moved and now some old geezer lives there and he doesn't invite us to go swimming. I wouldn't want to swim in a pool full of white, curly chest hairs anyways.

When class began, I practically melted on my way over to the computer. Veronica was asleep at her desk, Mason was in the bathroom, and Miranda was performing the ritualistic Daily Squeeze on Eleanor. She turned to me as I walked up and wrapped me in an anaconda-like grasp.

"Alright there," I wheezed. She pulled away quick, though.

"Ugh, you're slimy," she said.

"Sorry."

I turned my eyes to the ground, a little embarrassed. I can't stop myself from sweating so much on days like this, you know? Mom even thought about taking me to the doctor to get some medication to help it once but I was really against that idea. I just didn't want to have to take pills on a daily basis, or be worried about the heat index too much, or anything like that. Right now, more than anything, I just want to ride my bike and be free.

I really wanted to talk to Eleanor. Something was bugging me, like a dog nipping at my heels, and I don't quite know what it is. I feel like talking to her would just help, for some reason. Like Eleanor would have something wise to say about it. She was like a Greek Goddess. She could look at the stars and tell you what the weather was going to be like a week from now. Though I don't think that's what Greek Goddesses do. That would be a lame power, actually. But *still*. I sort of miss talking to her a bunch, too. Just me and her, alone. Though I guess in the group chat it wasn't all *that* alone. I mean, we only have English class together and I pass her on the stairs but that's about it. Every class is a blur, all in a build-up for English.

So now is the best time. Veronica is asleep, Mason is doing who-knows-what in the bathroom, (probably watching old SNL skits on his phone), and the only person sort of in the way is Miranda.

"Hey, Miranda," I said, "Why doesn't everyone get The Daily Squeeze?"

Comic Sans

"Not everyone is in our group, you big goof," she said.

"So? Don't they deserve it, too?" I said. Miranda thought about this for second.

"You know? You're right." And she bounded away and started giving everyone giant hugs. I made sure everyone was out of earshot and turned to Eleanor, biting my lip, wanting to talk to her but not even sure where to start.

We sat there in silence like that for a minute. I opened my mouth.

"So I –"

Suddenly, someone grabbed me from behind. I choked on my words and tore the hands away from me.

"I was thinking, you know, since you guys *are* my group and all, you still deserve more hugs so double squeezes!" Miranda squeaked. She ran over to Eleanor next and gave her a hug from behind. Eleanor kept working on the computer, but pat Miranda on the head with one hand.

"What were you saying, James?" Eleanor asked.

"Oh, I, um…." I rubbed my neck. It was a little sore. "I'm getting a job. At Smith's Gastro Pub." I said it so quick she might not have even heard me. I was practically farting out of my mouth. Just air and nonsense out of nervousness.

"Really? When do you begin? Like, when will you start working?" Eleanor asked, keeping her eyes on the screen.

"Um, I don't know," I said. I sort of regretted bringing it up. I was almost lying. "Actually, I haven't had my interview yet. But I will on Friday."

Katie Mlinek

"That's awesome!" She turned to me with a big smile. "Good luck! You're going to do great. I mean, really. They're going to love you."

"Yeah?" My voice cracked slightly. It kinda popped out of me. I didn't mean to sound like such a little pubescent boy but it just happened. "Whoops," I said. Eleanor giggled.

"Hey," she said, giving me a big smile again. "You're James Watterworth. Your voice can crack during the whole interview and they'll *still* love you."

That made my chest flutter, but then I started thinking. I mean, I feel like I tried my best during the Food Lion and Dollar Tree interviews, but something just felt off about the both of them. No one seemed like they were jumping up to hire me. Maybe Eleanor is wrong.

"Thanks," I said anyways.

"Do you have a special outfit that you wear for interviews?" she asked, giggling. "I've got this shoulder-padded blazer that my mom always makes me wear for important things, like internships, interviews, things like that. It's literally disgusting but she says that's the only reason why anyone takes me seriously during those sorts of things. Truly."

"Really? That's crazy! I just wear jeans and a T-shirt," I said. Which got me thinking again. What if it *did* make me look unprofessional? If the second the managers saw me, they wrote me off as another deadbeat and were just humoring me the entire interview? Or maybe I've just become overly paranoid about everything.

"So you basically wear the same thing as every other day?" Eleanor asked, laughing.

I laughed, too. "Pretty much."

Comic Sans

Veronica finally woke up, Mason meandered back from the bathroom, and Miranda practically collapsed into her seat, exhausted and red-faced from all the hugging. Our "private conversation" had barely been given a chance to even begin.

"Have any of you guys gotten your parts done yet?" Eleanor asked. They all shook their heads.

"I've been pretty busy working," Mason said.

"I just haven't done it," Veronica said.

"I've been skyping my dad," Miranda said.

"Really? Why? Where is he?" Eleanor asked.

"He's always traveling somewhere. He's a journalist. He's in Zimbabwe right now, reporting on that new species of frogs."

"That's so cool," Mason said.

"Well, thank goodness he's not in Iraq," Eleanor said.

Miranda nodded. "That's what my mom always says. Whenever she gets sad or misses him, we just go to the zoo and get fried ice cream for dinner."

"Dude, have you seen the Komodo dragon there?" Mason asked. "That thing is a beast. I mean, it's not like as big as a wildcat or anything, but I bet it could tear you up."

"My mom hates lizards," Miranda said.

"My mom's never even home," Veronica said.

"Why not?" Mason asked.

She just shrugged. "She's always at some bar with some guy. Or friends. My brother takes care of stuff, mostly. I can go a whole week without seeing her once."

"Oh, Veronica," Miranda said, "that's awful."

Katie Mlinek

Veronica shrugged again. "It's whatever."

"She still loves you though, right? I mean, even though my dad is never around, I know he still loves me."

"Wow, that's real tactful, Miranda," Mason said.

"I don't think she does," Veronica said. She didn't seem sad or upset at all. If anything, she seemed like she didn't care all that much. Or maybe she was just pretending.

"I understand, Veronica," Eleanor said. I looked at her in surprise. "Sometimes I feel like my parents don't really love me for me, you know? Sorry, that sounds awful and cheesy. But it's like...." She trailed off and looked off into the distance. "It's like they love who they *want* me to be, who they're trying to make me be, without really knowing me. Does that make any sense?"

"Dang, you guys are some serious people!" Mason said. "Am I in an AA meeting or an English class?"

"Sorry," Eleanor said.

"Don't be sorry," I said. "And shut up, Mason." I turned back to Eleanor. "I never asked, are you guys liking your new house okay, at least?" I really didn't know what to say about all that stuff she just said. I mean, I felt awful for Eleanor and all. I think she's probably right, and smart and brave for being able to say all that. But how am I supposed to respond to something like that? I can't. I'll take *any* other subject over really serious talk any day. So changing the subject is my only option.

Eleanor just shrugged. "I like it. I have a really nice room where I get space and stuff. But I hate the bird bath in our yard, though. Birds always poop in it and my parents make me clean it out."

"That sucks," I said. "My old neighbor down the street used to have a dog, and sometimes it came over and used the bathroom in our yard. My parents always made me clean it up because my neighbors never would, if they knew the dog, you know, *went*, and anyways, it always made me gag."

"Did you ever full on puke?" Eleanor asked, getting a little light in her eyes.

"Sorry to disappoint, but no," I said.

"Oh well," Eleanor said. "I love a good embarrassing puke story."

"That's disgusting," Veronica said.

"Oh, I have a really good one," Miranda said. She cleared her throat a little bit – dramatically, of course – and began. Veronica braced herself.

"I was at a wedding," Miranda said slowly, eyeing each of us. We were immediately enraptured. This was a side to Miranda none of us had seen before. "And I was young. Young*er*. I think seven. Well, let's see, it was in 2001, so –"

"Get on with it!" Mason said.

"Hold on! So I was seven. It was my cousin's wedding. It was in a fancy ballroom, and they had a quintet, and on every table, a platter of *fancy cookies*."

We all audibly gasped – jokingly, of course – though I think everyone was legitimately enjoying this little story time.

"I *love* cookies. I love cookies as much as I love hugs. Maybe even more."

We all sarcastically gasped again and tried not to laugh.

"So I ate tons of cookies. I ate cookies from three tables, I think. And, because I was seven, it was a little too much at once for me."

Katie Mlinek

"But now you could handle that just fine?" I asked, grinning.

"Of course she could, you silly, just keep listening," Eleanor said, grinning back.

Miranda paused and looked at all of us. Once she was sure we were done talking, she continued. "And I went up to my cousin, the *bride*, and tugged on her hand. She bent down to me and I puked right there, all over her and her dress!"

"I knew it!" Mason said. "I knew that's what was going to happen!"

"I'm pretty sure everyone guessed it, doofus," Veronica said.

We all laughed and Miranda laughed and sat back down.

"Hey," Veronica said once everyone had stopped laughing. We all looked at her. "I hope your dad comes back from Zimbabwe soon."

"Thanks." Miranda gave the most genuine smile I had ever seen. Not a hug-attack smile, not a I-just-said-a-crazy-thing-that-no-one-understood smile, but a real, deep-hearted one. And Veronica smiled right back.

"Guys, we've wasted a whole other class *again*," Eleanor said, looking at the clock.

"It'll be okay," I said. "You got the puke story you've always wanted today. How does it feel?"

"Pretty good, I guess." She laughed. "But seriously. Hamlet. Let's do this thing."

So we gathered around the computer a little closer and watched Eleanor do all the work.

Comic Sans

Chapter 18

So here's the deal. I've got fifty bucks from my grandma in Florida who I haven't seen for seven years and twenty from my Aunt Shirley from my last birthday. I never really spend money, so it's just sort of been lying around. But I'm going to get myself a suit. I really am. And I'll wear it to the Smith's Gastro Pub interview, and I'll look really professional and put-together and then they'll *have* to give me the job, they'll barely have any other choice.

The thing is, I don't want Mom or Dad to know. I ran it by Eleanor at the end of class and she got really excited. Like, *really* excited. She wanted to know all these details about the buttons and if I had good socks or matching shoes and more than I had even considered. At least I could talk to her about it. Mom and Dad, well – I just feel like they wouldn't want me spending money on a suit. I don't know why. They've both been too weird lately for me to feel safe running any idea by them. Mom might shoot it down before I even finish saying it. Dad would probably want to have a big conversation about putting my money in a bank and being financially responsible or something. Something really hypocritical like that.

But I *know* this is worth it. And when they say they don't remember me ever wearing it, I'll say Aunt Shirley sent it to me and I couldn't believe they didn't remember. Mom, Dad, and Aunt Shirley all have crap memories. Aunt Shirley once sent me a watch a week after my birthday because she forgot that she already sent me a tie and Mom made me send back the watch, though I would have preferred sending back the tie. Ties are all stiff and choke me more than Miranda's hugs. The watch was nice. But anyways, Mom and Dad barely remember what day it is so the long and short of it is that I'm not worried about that part.

I'll have to bike a really long ways to get to the closest consignment store. It's probably an hour or so. I've only biked into town once, to rent *The Blob* from the Blockbuster there, but now Blockbuster is closed and there's a Chipotle instead and I never watch movies anymore anyways.

I planned to go after school on Thursday, when Mom would be at a PTA meeting and Dad would be hanging out with his old trucker buddies at the local bar for Happy Hour and I'd have the suit in time for my interview the next day. When Thursday finally came, I grabbed the money and stuffed it in my pocket and headed out to the consignment store. It closed at five, and Mom and Dad would both get back around then anyways, so I had to leave the second school ended. Mom already said she'd be home after school all day on Friday, so she could take me to the interview no problem. Dad had his own interview to be a private trucker at some cookie factory an hour away. Mom ruffled both of our hair the other day during a random good mood spurt and called us her "Mangy Men," all unemployed and scraggly and the like. Dad had rolled his eyes at me and I had just laughed.

The ride there was alright. I had to bike along some bigger roads where cars go as fast as 60mph but for some reason I don't remember being scared the one other time I biked this far. It kinda freaked me out this time, though. All those lives rushing past me and with one slight turn of the wheel, I'd be splat along the concrete barrier forever. It's just weird to think about. Or how *I* could turn my wheel and be done with this world. I'm not suicidal in any way, really I'm not, I like living and all just fine, but when I remember stuff like that, it almost makes me feel better, in

Comic Sans

a way. That no matter what life does to me, and how much I don't know what it's all for, I'm choosing to still live it. And spend my entire seventy bucks in one go. Oh well.

By about the halfway point, my legs started to hurt something bad. It had been mostly uphill at that point, but the rest was all coasting and then I got there even faster than I expected. When I first walked into the store, all I noticed were girl's clothes. At first I thought I walked into the complete wrong place and I almost did the whole thing where you pretend like you forgot something in your car so you turn around to go get it. But then I saw a teeny little sign almost hidden by the dresses and skirts stacked to the ceiling that said, "Men's Clothes Upstairs." So I went up the winding staircase and there they were, a room full of suits.

I rifled through them quickly, just looking for ones that seemed like the right size to start. Already I felt exhausted. Maybe the exhaustion from the long bike ride was kicking in, but digging through all those clothes made my arms super tired. After the first rack, I felt ready to go home. I was suddenly grateful that Mom had done my clothes shopping all these years. This place smelled like Mrs. Cobbleson. That weird, old lady smell really gets to me.

Finally I found one that looked like the right size, but when I checked the tag it said it was extra small, so I must have been wrong, and it was $110. Is it just me, or is that an insane amount of money for a suit? I thought they'd be around $30 and I'd have money to spare for French fries or something. I mean, $110 can't be consignment. I thought consignment meant "super cheap." At least that was my understanding of it. Sometimes I feel like the whole world gets together to decide weird social constructs and I'm the only one who didn't attend.

So I kept digging through all the clothes. They had it split up into time periods in one room, suits from the 40s and 50s and so on, but they really all looked the same to me. And the shoes – I hadn't even *thought* about shoes – lined all of the walls. They looked nice on the outside, some of them, clean and sharp and polished, but if you looked inside, you'd see all the crummy padding or whatever peeling up and flaking away like paint. I stuck my hand inside one of them just to see what it was like and it felt moist, as if some sweaty guy had just taken them off. I looked around the store quick to make sure no one had seen me do it. No one was there. So then I smelled my hand, and it smelled like feet and I sighed and went back to digging through suits.

While I looked through the clearance rack (if consignment stores have stuff to put on clearance racks, shouldn't it just be free at that point?), I noticed through the window that it had started raining outside. I just kept on searching, but then I realized that meant I'd have to bike back through the rain. Ugh. I was mad both at myself and the weather – the weather for doing this to me, and myself for not having the foresight to check it.

"Finding everything okay?"

I turned, startled to see another human being, and nodded meekly. "Yes, thanks," I said quickly. What if she was standing there while I smelled my hand? I suddenly felt really embarrassed without even being sure she had seen me.

She smiled and started looking through the clothes, too, as if checking it for dust or something. It was making me uncomfortable, to be honest. How she was sticking around and all. I kept glancing at her out of the corner of my eye and felt super self-conscious about everything. How my hand smelled, how sweaty I must smell, even how the smell of the rain outside was starting to seep in and make all these smells stronger. But why should it all even matter? I'm here on a mission. But I had looked through all the suits and found nothing. Only the navy blue one that turned out to not even have been navy blue. There

Comic Sans

were other ones, suits so gross even I could recognize them as being ugly. What respectable man is going to wear a sequined rainbow suit? One had Celtic swirls, one had more shoulder padding than shoulder, and one had a zipper instead of buttons. So I decided to start back from the beginning, clear my head a little, and look again. Maybe I had missed something.

This time as I looked through all the suits, I checked only the price tags. I felt more and more dismayed each minute. They were all $100, $120, some even as much as $200. All I had was a measly $70 that I had "saved up."

And then suddenly, I found the one. *The one*. I've seen those wedding dress shopping shows with my mom – against my will – where the girl starts crying and the mother starts crying and soon everyone is crying and they're all like, "this is the one, this is the one, great googly moogly, this is the one!" It was kind of like that, except I didn't cry at all or scream "great googly moogly!" I found it just as the woman left, bringing all her bad juju or whatever with her. It was $65 exactly, leaving me just enough wiggle room for tax. It was tan, which I could compromise on, and it looked like just the right size.

I pulled the jacket part over my T-shirt and it fit perfectly. If that fit so well, I just assumed the pants would fit the same. I tumbled down the stairs and the woman was at the register, so I slid the money over as quickly as I could and didn't even get a bag for it. I hopped on my bike and it wasn't even raining that bad. I felt giddy. Which made me feel silly, in a way. I was no better than all those girls on reality TV shows. The thought sickened me a little, but it couldn't dim my delight at finding something so perfect and so cheap. I would look really sharp and get the job and make money and it would be like I hadn't spent anything at all.

Like I said, the rain had practically stopped. It was just a pathetic drizzle now and it barely bothered me. My suit wasn't getting too wet or anything, but I didn't worry too much, though

Katie Mlinek

I *did* regret not taking a bag. I went back with my suit slung victoriously over the handlebars of my bike.

Comic Sans

Chapter 19

The one thing I wasn't expecting as I biked back was how muddy it would be from that one little downpour. Mud was splattering onto my bike and even hitting the bottom of my jeans. Already I was worrying about how to get them into the washer without Mom noticing. Though I guess I could come up with some weird lie about that, too. How there was a giant mud puddle right outside the school doors or something.

    I had just entered my neighborhood again, which I knew because I've lived here for so long, but the average person would probably have no idea. It's not like most normal neighborhoods with a nice sidewalk system and a big embossed sign with the name "Quarry Lake" or "Peach Hill" or even "Everyone Here Sucks Town," but it's a neighborhood nonetheless. Huge pine trees are the only real border around it, but a handful of them got a weird disease last winter and died so there's not even a complete border anymore. They're really big, though. Not like the Rockefeller Christmas tree, but definitely at least three times the size of the average Christmas tree.

    Once I passed through the tree border, I zipped down the road towards my house. I had to go through the rich part first. When I saw Eleanor's bird bath house, my heart skipped a beat. Somehow I had forgotten, in all my huff to get a suit and an interview and stuff, that she lived so close to me. I didn't want to look at her house as I went by – really, I didn't – but the windows are so *huge* and so clear they must be washed twice a day. I could see a TV flashing CNN in one of the rooms, and in the room right next to it there was Eleanor, eating around a dinner table with her family. There were two younger girls sitting at the table with her. I didn't even *know* she had younger sisters. I turned my head and started biking even faster.

    I felt really bad for looking. I couldn't stop myself, I mean the windows made the house look so bright that you would think it was on fire or something. But I felt like I had peeped into something I shouldn't, a moment from Eleanor's personal life. After I was a good ways down the road, it occurred to me what was so strange and uncomfortable about it, though. None of them were talking. Eleanor and her parents and her two younger sisters were silently eating their food.

    And it made me think, too, about how Eleanor doesn't talk all that much about her personal life or anything. I mean, she does *some* times, but not in the way most teenagers do. Most kids talk about how their cousins are wrong about everything or how their mom gives them no space or their cats scratch them too much. Eleanor only mentions little things about her life, tiny details that probably no one in the world would ever notice. Like how cold her bathroom gets when it's windy.

    Though she did tell me that one story about the cooking class she had to take. Man, her parents were super intense about that. Eleanor didn't mention that it was with some famous chef or anything. She's way too humble for something like that. And her parents seemed to have no idea that she hated it. Why didn't she tell them?

    I felt bad suddenly for sneaking behind my parents' backs and all just to get a suit. They're not like Eleanor's parents. They don't hand me everything on a silver platter and force me to take

Comic Sans

it. And here I am, acting like some stupid oppressed teenage boy. I hate myself.

The sidewalk began on Edmunson Street, so I moved off the road and onto the curb. But there was a huge mud puddle right there, and my tires skidded, and suddenly my suit unfolded and caught under the wheels and fell off the handlebar and the laws of gravity were against me in every way possible and the suit sunk under the tires just as they ground themselves into the mud and the dirt and the who-knows-what and suddenly there it was, my sixty-five dollar suit crumpled stained and ruined against the curb. I rolled off my bike and noticed a long scratch going up my leg, blood just starting to peek through. I stood there and looked at my bike. I looked at my suit. I didn't move.

I looked back over at my crumpled suit on the ground. I pinched the corner of it and lifted it up, letting the brown, mucky water drip off of it.

"Are you okay, sweetie?"

I turend my head and there was Mrs. Cobbleson. She was standing right outside her front door and rushed over to me.

"Did you get cut up anywhere?" she asked.

"No," I said, "probably just some bruises."

"Would you like a cup of tea? You took a bad spill there, could use some warming up," she said.

"No, thank you," I said, trying to brush her off. I looked around the street to see if anyone else had seen my tumble. Then it occurred to me that if anyone had, they probably just pulled their curtains a little tighter. That's the sort of crap people do in this neighborhood. "It's very nice of you to offer, Mrs. Cobbleson," I said.

"My front door is always open if you change your mind," she said.

Katie Mlinek

I thanked her again and waved my goodbye, righting my bike again. My suit was still sopping wet by the time I got home, and I had no idea what to do with it – do I wash it and risk Mom seeing it? Or hide it in my room somewhere where it might soak everything?

I got home in plenty of time before Mom and Dad, and decided to wrap the suit in a grocery bag and stick it in the back of my closet with all my foul-smelling shoes. My soaked suit was so heavy that it immediately crushed all of my shoes. I noticed, on the floor, next to the bag, this old squishy ball that's painted to look like a soccer ball. The paint was starting to chip away and you could see the foam underneath it, but I decided I didn't want to throw it away. It's stupid, but it really took me back for some reason to when I was a kid. I had this best friend named Jimmy Litzinger in elementary school, until his family had to move away in fourth grade because his dad was in the military or something. Anyways, I won the soccer ball from the classroom prize box for getting 100% on my vocabulary test, and during class Jimmy and I would roll it between our desks with our feet and hope the teacher didn't notice. The teacher never did. We were really careful. All of the kids in the class knew, and sometimes they would keep a really close tally on how well we were doing. And whenever one of us didn't catch it, or kicked it in the wrong directions, the other kids weren't jerks and kept it or anything. They'd always roll it back. I liked that. I miss things being like that.

Comic Sans

Chapter 20

The first thing Eleanor asked me the next day was if I got the suit or not.

Then the fire alarm rang.

Which was fine by me, even though it was hot as hell outside and the air conditioner was actually semi-working in the building today. But we all lined up and filed into the hallway and Eleanor was given the "special" duty of turning all the lights out. So I didn't have to answer her question, and I crossed my fingers that in all this hubbub she would forget about it. She turned off the lights and fell in at the back of the line and we went outside into the heat. If someone had an ice cream cone – which they wouldn't anyways since it's the middle of the school day – but *if* they did, it would have melted the second it crossed the doors.

My English teacher led us outside to the tennis courts and we lined up against the side. I was standing in between two kids I didn't know that well, so I sat down, suddenly exhausted out of my mind. I really was tired. My eyes were starting to burn a little and as I sat there more, it started to get hard to focus my eyes. *That* sort of tired. So I closed my eyes and leaned my head against the fence.

The thing with these fire drills is that kids don't actually stay in lines for long. I never really know what it is that makes fire drills take so long where everyone's just hanging around, standing for a good fifteen minutes waiting for *something*, but anyways teenagers can only stay in a line for so long.

I kept my eyes closed and started to feel drowsy from the heat. I sort of started to fall asleep, in a not-asleep-way. You know when you're just so overcome with exhaustion that you sort of forget where you are and you have these weird, hazy dreams? And they make sense at the time, and suddenly five minutes later you wake up and realize where you are but you feel half in that dream world that you can't remember anymore? It's a strange phenomenon. But anyways, that happened.

So I'm having a weird dream and stuff, I think it was about having boiled carrots for dinner or something, and I wake up and Eleanor's sitting next to me against the fence.

"Mason wanted to kick you awake but I wouldn't let him," she said. She had sweat starting to bead on the top of her forehead and she wiped it away with her forearm. "It was exhausting work."

I laughed. "Thanks." I rubbed my eyes, still a little groggy, and looked around at everything. Teachers and students and cafeteria ladies were just milling around. Our English class looked like they had just emerged from a dangerous expedition in the Amazon jungle. I could see the whole thing now: Mrs. Desarrollee guides us into the jungle, Mason tries to take the lead, points us in the wrong direction, we get lost for a week. A couple of kids fall prey to jaguars or whatever lives in jungles but most of us make it through okay. We eat bugs under sticks. Drink water from leaves. And by the time we make it out of the jungle, half of everyone loves each other and half of everyone hates each other. Right now, sweat was dripping out of them faster than gravity could pull it downwards and some were practically panting like dogs.

"How long was I asleep?" I asked Eleanor.

Comic Sans

She shrugged. "Like ten minutes. More than five. Maybe seven. Yeah, seven."

I laughed a little. "Okay. Seven minutes exactly. Good to know."

I was starting to wake up a little bit more and sit up straighter. Kids were practically shoveling sweat off of their foreheads now. I looked down at my shirt and saw that it was soaked. It was embarrassing, and I had no way of covering it up. But when I looked over at Eleanor, she had these giant sweat stains under each of her arms and I felt a little bit better. Like we were in this torment together.

"So," she said, "you didn't get a chance to tell me about your suit!"

"Yeah, that," I said. I rubbed the back of my neck. "Well, thing is, you know how it rained yesterday? I dropped it in the mud right as I got home. And I don't know how to get mud stains out. It's ruined."

"Oh no!" Eleanor said. "Oh, James! That's awful! I'm so sorry!"

I felt weirdly relieved, telling her. As if I had been holding it in a tad too long, like a burp, and it makes your stomach feel all weird. But letting it out is a bit better.

"Yeah," I said, "T-shirt and jeans it is for me."

"Your interview is today, right?" Eleanor asked.

I nodded.

Eleanor jumped up and then sat back down again. "Sorry. Sorry, sorry. I just realized something. You have a toothbrush, right?"

Katie Mlinek

I laughed. "Um, yeah. I have a toothbrush. Why, what are you trying to say?" I pushed her arm playfully and she laughed.

"No, no, nothing. Nothing like that. But listen, I know how you can save your suit. They had a special on TV once, when I was at a beach house and didn't really want to go to bed and there was nothing else to watch."

I remembered seeing her and her family the night before and felt embarrassed all over again. I sort of wanted to ask about her sisters but it would just be too hard to explain how I even knew they existed.

"So is there caked-on mud? Like, is it dry?" she asked.

"Yeah. I checked this morning. Part of it is dry and part is still wet."

"Okay. Okay, okay. So. Just kick off all the dry stuff, get rid of it that way. It's okay if part of it is wet. You need to take your toothbrush and wash it and put a little bit of laundry detergent on it and scrub all the muddy parts. Don't let it get too wet! Then the mud might spread more and there wouldn't be much you could do. But yeah, just gently scrub it. It'll take some time but you might be able to get it done before your interview after school today. You can wash it normally after scrubbing it."

"Really?" I felt another wave of relief wash over me. "Thank you so much! You remember all this just from a TV show? Are you sure it works? It sounds like magic. I don't know any of this stuff, though. But I trust you. I'll do it the second I get home." I felt like hugging her, but it wasn't the time or place and we'd just get gross sweat all over each other and maybe she'd never want to hug me again. I was so excited, not only that there was a chance I could save my suit but just that Eleanor had the thought to help me out in this way.

"I have an idea," I said, "how about we work out a system over the summer where you wash all my clothes with these

Comic Sans

brilliant tricks of yours and I sit around eating grapes or eclairs or something?"

She laughed. "Nice try, silly. But I'm going to be leaving right when school ends for a leadership conference. It's in Denver, and once that's over I'm going to spend a month with my grandparents. So I'll be gone most of the summer."

"Really? That's great, Eleanor. That's really great," I said.

Not great. Not great no matter what way you look at it. Denver is practically across the entire country. Now that I know she lives so close, I was looking forward to breaking that barrier where we can go over to each other's houses and hang out and stuff. We could go biking together and get ice cream afterwards if the ice cream truck ever came by, like little kids. I'd get a deformed Spiderman popsicle and she'd get a big-headed Dora one. And then we'd find a nice little grove of pine trees somewhere that would become our spot and we'd meet up there late, without our parents knowing, on nights when they call for meteor showers. I hadn't even realized quite consciously how much I'd been entertaining these ideas in my head. And now that she said she was leaving, I felt sillier than ever. For thinking I had some right or something to spend my whole summer with her. Of course she was going to be doing something. Something worthwhile and productive and resume-worthy. Of course.

"You're going to love it, Eleanor." I smiled. "I'm so sure you will."

Students and teachers started to move back towards the school and we soon followed. Our class was in the very back, so by the time we got halfway across the tennis court, there was already a huge mob of kids trying to squeeze through the small entrance. Everyone was being jostled quite a bit and at one point Eleanor grabbed onto my arm as someone smashed into her.

"Stick by me," I said, in a joke-y, macho-man kind of way.

Katie Mlinek

She scoffed. "You're the one who needs to stick by me," she said.

I laughed. "You're probably right. Hey, this will be good training for when you leave this summer, though. Being in Denver all by yourself. You gotta build muscle. I won't be there to protect you."

She looked down. I thought she was going to laugh, but she didn't. "Yeah," she said, "I'll be mostly on my own for a while. I will miss you, though. But just a little. Just this much." She held up two fingers so close they were practically touching and laughed, getting a little red in the face.

My insides burst into a million fireworks.

Comic Sans

Chapter 21

When I got home, I immediately set to work on my suit. I recited answers to standard interview questions over and over again in my head, and I was suddenly thankful for the Food Lion and Dollar Tree ones. They both asked relatively similar questions, so I won't have to stutter or think as much this time around. I can focus on being laid back and relaxed and calm and cool and collected and not overthink anything or forget the question in the midst of thinking – oh my gosh, what if I *do* forget, what if I have to ask him to repeat the question and he glares at me and – okay. Maybe I'm a tad nervous.

I said one last goodbye to my toothbrush, which I had probably had for way too long anyways, and set to work scrubbing my suit. It was peaceful, in a weird way. Mom and Dad both weren't home, which is weird since they said they would be, but I liked the scrubbing toothbrush as the only sound in the entire house. I got really into it. It was detailed work, like looking over really long and complicated chemistry problems. It did get a little tiring, after a while.

Time kept creeping on and I kept scrubbing away with my toothbrush and detergent. My suit didn't look like it was getting any cleaner at all. It was mostly just getting slippery, to tell you the truth. But I figured Eleanor must have known what she was talking about and when I was done, I plopped it in the washer and turned it on.

Two hours later, after washing and drying the whole thing, it looked perfect. It not only looked like it did when I bought it yesterday, which was miraculous in and of itself, but it even lost that gross old-person-mothball smell that the consignment store clothes all had. It was soft and clean and I'll be honest, I even held it against my face once it came out of the dryer, it was so warm.

But the thing is, Mom and Dad weren't home yet and we had to leave in forty-five minutes. They both said they'd be home. Both of them. So they must be somewhere together or something. Why didn't they find a phone booth to call our landline or something? This is where having a cellphone would be *really* helpful right about now. Ugh. There probably aren't any phone booths in this entire state.

I decided to start cleaning up my room because I vaguely remembered Mom saying something about it needing to be fully straightened and vacuumed and stuff by Saturday. I don't know why she gets these sudden, desperate urges for everything to be completely clean. It's not like they ever correspond with guests coming over or holidays or anything. We never do anything fun at our house. It's just a matter of her losing her mind and thinking that somehow a clean house will make up for it.

So anyways, I half-heartedly started cleaning up my room but I kept half an eye on the time. It kept on ticking by and still no click of the front door opening. Did Mom and Dad not care? Had they just forgotten all about me and this interview? But I immediately waved the idea out of my head. There was no way Mom and Dad could just *forget* about me. I'm their only son, I'm the only thing they have to keep track of. And this was my last chance of getting a summer job. I don't know of any other jobs available anywhere else in this entire town or state or even nation for that matter, and I need this job. I need somewhere to be other than this house and school. I need money because we obviously don't have enough. I just need this. And Mom and Dad are still nowhere to be found.

Comic Sans

Finally we came to five minutes before I had to go. By this point, I was losing it completely. There was no other possibility other than Mom and Dad having forgotten about me. But could I reschedule the interview? Mom's the one who had given me Smith's phone number, which I don't have now, of course, so I can't call to say that I can't make it. And after all this ridiculous effort I've put into this suit...I can't even use it. They'll write me off as a deadbeat without even seeing me because I'll be a no-show.

There had to be something I could do. If I biked there, I'd be an hour late to the interview. That would probably look worse than just not showing up at all. I could call when Mom and Dad get home and blame it on them entirely. But then I'll seem like an untrustworthy employee and why would they expect me to be able to show up to work on time if I can't even make it to an interview? Of course they wouldn't. The only thing I could do was find someone else to drive me.

But I don't know anyone. I mean, I *know* people in the neighborhood, but I hardly know anyone well enough to ask them to drive me somewhere lickity-split. Everyone in the immediate vicinity of my house is old and I doubt they'd be able to drive me somewhere on such short notice, or even drive at all. I can't remember half of anyone's names. But then I remembered – Eleanor's right down the street.

I threw on my suit and grabbed my resume that had been sitting nice and clean and safe at the top of my bookshelf. I gave it a once-over and folded it up and put it on an inside pocket of my suit – it had an inside pocket! – and hopped on my bike. The ground was muggy, from the humidity or the rain yesterday I couldn't tell, and it started to squirt up mud at the bottom of my pants. But I had to go.

I biked faster than I think I ever have in my entire life and ran up to Eleanor's doorbell so quick that I didn't even realize

Katie Mlinek

how rude it was for me to just leave my bicycle lying in their yard next to their bird bath. I rang the doorbell and the tall woman that I recognized as Eleanor's mom came to the door.

A look of near-disgust (but probably just surprise) came over her face. "Yes?" she asked.

I panted. "Hello…Mrs…Iding…my name is.…" I took a huge gulp of air and wiped the sweat away from my face. "I'm –"

"You're that boy down the street in Eleanor's school, right?" she said. "Hold on."

She turned around and walked all lady-like to call for Eleanor from the bottom of the staircase. Even though she was shouting from downstairs, there was something so formal and restrained in her voice that I cringed. When my mom shouts for people, she really hollers. Not all dainty and polite like Mrs. Iding.

Eleanor came down the stairs just as gracefully as her mom had walked up to them, and smiled when she saw me at the door.

"James! Is this your suit? It looks really nice," she said.

"Yeah, this is it. But the thing is, my parents haven't come home yet and they said they would be. They should have been home hours ago. I think they forgot about me or something. And I have to leave to get to my interview on time right now. And there's no one who can drive me."

"You want me to? But James, I can't drive," she said.

"I know, I know."

"What, you want my parents to drive you?" She looked at me with her eyebrows raised.

"I…no, I.…" I faltered. "I guess I didn't think this through."

Comic Sans

What *was* I thinking? Why did I rush over so quickly, as if she could do something? Why couldn't I just let this interview go?

"No, it's okay. You said it's at Smith's Gastro Pub, right? Let me just ask my mom real quick. She said we were going grocery shopping today anyways." Eleanor gave me a sympathetic smile and went into another room, leaving me standing on the steps right outside her open door.

I stood there and looked around at everything. It was a nice yard, the more I looked at it. I could see past the bird bath and all now that I tried. But boy, my heart was pounding so fast I was starting to feel dizzy.

Finally, Eleanor came back to the door. Her shoes were right next to it and she immediately bent down to put them on.

"Yeah, we can take you," she said, looking up at me. She finished tying her shoes. "My mom is just getting ready really quick. We can get in the car now, though."

We walked around to the side door for her garage and inside was the biggest, most expensive looking car I had ever seen. I slid into the back seat and ran my hand over the smooth leather. It felt just as luxurious as car commercials make fancy, expensive cars seem. Who knew that it wasn't false advertising all this time?

Eleanor sat in the front seat and we sat in silence for a bit.

She bit her lip. "She'll be coming out any second – oh! There she is." Eleanor smiled at her mom as she got in the car. Her mom turned the car on, opened the garage door, and pulled it out.

"Ellie says you have an interview at Smith's Gastro Pub?" she asked, looking at me through the rearview mirror. It made me uncomfortable, only seeing her eyes. "I wish you lots of luck. We go there all the time, don't we, Ellie? Very nice restaurant."

"Thank you," I said, "and thank you so much for giving me this ride last minute. I really appreciate it." My voice was so loud

Katie Mlinek

that I was hurting my own ears. I just felt so awkward I couldn't control it. It boomed more than I wanted it to for such a compact car.

"I know this was rushed," I continued, "and it's not the usual situation that a boy shows up to a girl's house wearing a suit for." I laughed at my own joke just to break the silence and then immediately felt like crawling under the seat. I considered hopping out of the car, too, but I wouldn't want Eleanor to have to see something as terrible as that. They both just looked at each other and I swear, I could smell the disapproval in Eleanor's mom. And man, if I was losing it this much, now, the interview wouldn't be much better.

We sat in silence for the rest of the way there. Even though Smith's Gastro Pub is located in the corner of the shopping center parking lot, it's a classy joint. But the shopping center is called Newman Square. How many shopping centers named Newman Square do you think exist in America alone? A thousand. Not that I know for sure, but I have a feeling I'm right.

Anyways, Smith's is right dab in the corner. One time, when I was driving past it, I saw a Lamborghini in its parking lot. Mom guessed it belonged to whoever owned the restaurant, like the financial backer guy, and I told her they aren't called "financial backer guys." I don't think she listened. And right now, thinking about Mom literally makes my blood boil. Like, blood starts to rush through my skin and I can feel it, I really can.

This has been the biggest lose-lose situation I think I've ever experienced. I feel like I'm getting away with murder. But I'm getting here late (though only like ten minutes which isn't *horrible*, I guess), and Mom and Dad definitely don't care about me enough to remember me or this interview that we've had planned for ages now, and Eleanor's mom probably never wants me going anywhere even near the sidewalk outside their house for the next year, at least.

Comic Sans

She pulled into the parking lot of Smith's Gastro Pub and stopped right outside the front doors. I got out of the car, talking on the whole way out.

"Thank you so much, Mrs. Iding, you have no idea what this means to me, I really appreciate it more than I can –"

"It's really no problem at all, happy to help," Mrs. Iding said. She didn't smile at all though, and I knew she was only saying it to be polite. Eleanor gave me a small wave and mouthed, "good luck!" and they drove away.

Man. I'm such a blubbering idiot.

Katie Mlinek

Chapter 22

A girl in her late twenties greeted me at the podium. "Hello, welcome to Smith's Gastro Pub. How many of you are there today?"

"Um, just one," I said.

"Do you have a reservation?"

"No, I –"

"Okay, follow me," she said, pulling out a menu.

"Wait, wait," I said. "I'm actually here for an interview. Not to eat." Boy, I felt stupid. She just said everything so fast I couldn't register it.

"Oh, you're the kid Mr. Rosenwood told me about!" she said, rushing back to the podium and putting the menu away. "Here, follow me, but this way." She turned left and from there took a dizzying amount of turns. I completely lost my sense of direction. I had no idea there could be so many hallways in a restaurant. Finally, she stopped in front of a closed door.

"Is that where mister...?"

"Rosenwood, yes. He should be in there. Just knock. And good luck!" She gave me another small smile before taking off back through the maze of hallways. I smoothed out my resume, making sure it hadn't gotten too crinkled, and knocked on the door.

"Come in," a voice said. I opened the door and it was, surprisingly, a very young-looking guy. Maybe as old as the waitress who brought me here. He wore a pinstripe suit, and if the restaurant had been more Italian, I might have thought he was a part of some mafia.

I walked into the room and sat down at the chair waiting in front of the desk. I could feel my fingers trembling no matter how hard I tried to control them, holding them in a clasped position.

"You must be James, correct?" he asked.

I nodded.

"Nice to meet you. My name is Mr. Rosenwood, and I'm the owner of this place. I'm not here often, I'm more of the financial backer guy, but I'm in charge of hiring people."

I nodded again. What am I supposed to say in situations like this? I waited for him to keep talking, but he didn't.

"Okay," I finally said, "Cool." I nodded again, so that he could tell I got it. I was starting to feel like a bobblehead.

"You're fifteen minutes late," he said.

"Yes, I'm so sorry. I got here as fast as I could," I said.

"It's funny," Mr. Rosenwood said, forcing a laugh, "most people get here fifteen minutes early. So, did you bring a resume? I believe I told your mother to bring one when I called."

I perked up. I didn't know he had called Mom, and she didn't tell me he said anything. I'm glad I had it on me anyways.

"Here you are," I said, sliding it towards him.

Katie Mlinek

He took it and sat still for a long time, looking it over. It was starting to make me really antsy. After a while I noticed the clock ticking behind his desk and then I just couldn't get that sound out of my head, I really couldn't. It was driving me almost crazy.

Finally he let out a big sigh. I held mine in.

"This looks good," he said, tossing it back on his desk and folding his hands. "Thanks for bringing it in."

"You're welcome, sir," I said. It felt weird calling him "sir," though. He really looked young. Like twenty-five or something. I feel like only people with gray hair deserve to be called "sir." But I couldn't stop myself. It was like a weird compulsion, probably out of near-desperation.

"Well, James…what was your last name again? Waddle-something?"

"Watterworth, sir." My insides were squirming, in an anxious sort of way. Like my intestines were having a temper tantrum disco party in my stomach.

"James Watterworth! Yes, it's quite the name."

"I do my best, sir." My awkwardness was killing me. This is what I get for making Eleanor's mom drive me. It would have been so much better if I just called and explained why I didn't show up and rescheduled it. I way overcomplicated it. Now my nerves were shot and my brain was shot and my chance at getting this job was *definitely* shot.

"So tell me a little bit about yourself," Mr. Rosenwood asked.

"Well, I like working with others," I said. I felt better about that one. I had practiced this. I was regaining *some* control.

Mr. Rosenwood nodded. "I understand that. I really do. I feel just the same way. People ask me all the time, 'how is it that

Comic Sans

you're able to work with others so well?' And do you want to know what the secret is? I'll let you in on it." He leaned forward and put his hands, still folded, onto the table. "Good shoes."

I nodded, but was completely taken by surprise. "Yeah. Definitely," was all I could think to say.

"It really is true. The fact of the matter is that people judge you for that kind of stuff. If they see that you can take good care of your shoes, they'll know that you'll take good care of them. It's that simple." He leaned back in his chair, clearly proud of his incredible insight. I felt more and more dismayed each second. First, I was hardly able to get my own words in edgewise; second, this guy was a nutjob. Then I looked down at my shoes. They were all muddy from my frantic bike ride earlier. I felt any sense of hope slip away quick and salty like sweat.

"So, what's your greatest motto in life?" he asked.

That one threw me for a loop. It wasn't a question I've ever been asked before. Or had expected to be asked, for that matter.

"Um, never give up," I said. Mr. Rosenwood closed his eyes and nodded his head slowly.

"Well here, we believe in a little something called teamwork. Ever heard the phrase, 'teamwork makes the dream work?' That's our little employee motto. It's not about letting failure happen. Good work should be the end goal." Mr. Rosenwood stared at me. The stripes on his suit were starting to hurt my eyes.

"I definitely agree, sir. Definitely," I said. I think sucking up will be my only saving grace now.

"Your mom said a similar motto as you, it's quite funny," he said.

"My mom?"

Katie Mlinek

"Ah, actually, that brings me to a point I wanted to make. I'm sure you realize that your mother can't get the job if you do, and vice versa. We just aren't in the position to accept two new employees right now. Though I will say we generally hire slightly older employees. Of course, I told her all this at her interview last week," Mr. Rosenwood said.

I shook my head and looked at the blank wall behind him. I just couldn't bring myself to look at him. Mom interviewed here? That must be why she was so weird about me wanting to interview here, too. Why would she do this to me? Purposefully create competition between us? And was she secretly looking to get a job? Was she secretly looking to take *my* job? Is this why she didn't come home to take me to the interview on time?

The thing is, Mom tells us everything every day – so much stuff that Dad and I often tune it out. How her hair got messy in a bunch of wind, a horrible driver on the highway, how hungry she was before lunch. But this is not something she's mentioned at the dinner table.

"That's understandable," I said. Even though all of a sudden I hardly understood anything at all.

"Well, thank you very much for the resume, again. I'll make sure to look this over some more. It was nice to meet you today, James. I'll call you sometime."

I stood up and walked over to shake his hand. He gestured to the door and I let myself out. I went down the hallway and took a right, then a couple of lefts before another right, and before I knew it, I was completely lost. I had walked past a bathroom, a row of private dining rooms, and I think two kitchens before giving up. *Two.* The people I walked by all looked very busy or important, so I didn't bother asking anyone for directions. Besides, it would just make me seem silly. Not knowing how to do something as simple as walk out of a restaurant. I bet that crazy guy designed this place, because it made absolutely no sense.

Comic Sans

I was just thinking about what I'd like to say to him when, as luck had it, I walked straight back into Mr. Rosenwood.

"Still here? Did you forget something?" he asked.

"I think I took a wrong turn somewhere," I said.

Mr. Rosenwood stopped a waitress hurrying by. "Can you please show this young man to the front door?" he asked. She nodded, he thanked her, and finally I was led to the front door.

And suddenly I realized – how was I going to get home?

Chapter 23

I can't believe myself. After all that frantic fuss about getting myself here and now I have no way of getting home. What was I thinking, all this time? Was I even thinking at all? I've messed this whole thing up. It sounds simple: get job, make money, be happy. But this has ended up being the most complicated mess I've ever created for myself. It's all my fault.

Though I guess I couldn't have known I had no chance anyways because my own stupid mother interviewed here before me. Does she not trust Dad to get a job soon? Or do we need the money right now that badly? The only thing I can be certain about right now is that she's the last person I want to see for the rest of the day – maybe the rest of the whole week. How could she? I mean, really – *how could she?*

I stuck my hands in my pocket and started wandering around the shopping center. It was pretty busy today, people carrying twenty bags of groceries and dragging kids into stores and parking over every line in the whole lot. I found a penny on the ground and picked it up. This, this penny, is all my life savings right about now.

"*James!*" I turned my head and saw Mom, driving slowly alongside the sidewalk with the window rolled down. "Your friend's mom told me you were here," she said.

Comic Sans

I turned back, put the penny in my pocket, and kept walking.

"Cut it out, James, just get in the car."

If there was on thing, one small tiny thing I could be sure of right now, it's that she deserved this. I walked slightly faster.

"Listen, I'm sorry, okay? Please get in the car, we can talk this over."

"You're blocking other cars," I said. And she really was – there were already two cars driving slowly behind her, trying to get around.

"I am not going anywhere until you get in this car."

I shrugged and kept going. I was enjoying this a little bit, to tell you the truth. It's nice to be so completely innocent and in the right. Normally I'm always the one who's done something wrong, but it's nice to have the tables turned. I remember once, maybe eight years ago, I promised to clean my room before the Fourth of July and didn't because I was playing soccer in the street with some older kids and Mom didn't let me eat a hot dog – and I love hot dogs – or stay up for the fireworks. I was devastated. My room wasn't all that messy, either.

"James Michael Watterworth." Uh-oh. Pulling out the full name. "I am your *mother*. I am not perfect, but I will not leave without you and until we fix this. I'm so, *so* sorry I didn't get home in time to take you to the interview. And you have no way of getting back home unless I take you. So just…just cut it out, and get in the car. Please."

There were five cars behind Mom now. The second one in line started honking its horn like crazy. People kept turning their heads to see what was going on, and just to stop the stupid commotion, I got into the car. I slammed the door shut.

Katie Mlinek

"Thank you," Mom huffed. She started driving faster and pulled out of the parking lot. "Put your seat belt on."

Begrudgingly, I did. We drove down the road in silence. I could tell Mom was trying to think of what to say. Whatever it was, I didn't really want to hear it. I wondered how Dad was enjoying his Happy Hour with his old trucker buddies.

Suddenly, Mom took a shrieking right turn. I grabbed onto my seatbelt in case we reached G-forces and kept my head firmly against the headrest.

"Sorry," she said. "I just had an idea." She came to a halting stop in a Dairy Queen parking lot. I didn't even know this Dairy Queen was here, but I got out of the car with Mom.

"C'mon, let's get milkshakes," she said.

Mom ended up not even getting a milkshake. She ordered a fancy sundae with a warm brownie at the bottom and wet nuts and hot fudge and even a freaking fake cherry on top. Me, I just wanted mint chocolate chip. As a milkshake.

We sat down at a sticky, padded booth that had never been cleaned properly in its entire existence and watched the other cars zip by on the road. Mom folded her napkin into a tiny square and kept dabbing her mouth between bites of ice cream. She kept squeezing and unsqueezing the napkin.

"Your suit looks nice. I don't think I've seen it before."

I shrugged. "Aunt Shirley," I muttered. We sat in silence some more. I stirred my milkshake.

"So tell me what's going through your head right now," she said.

I shrugged again. "Nothing."

Comic Sans

She raised her eyebrows. "Well, I know that can't be true. C'mon. Just tell me."

I shrugged again. To explain everything I was feeling right now seemed too exhausting. I really didn't want to. I stirred around the chocolate chips in my milkshake. I can't believe she got a fancy sundae.

"I didn't get home in time because I was at my own interview as a receptionist for that legal firm in the city," she said.

"Oh, yeah?" I said. "And did you interview at the Dollar Tree and Food Lion, too?"

Mom sighed. "So you're mad I didn't tell you—"

"Mr. Rose-face told me."

Mom sighed again and ate the cherry on top of her sundae. But I know she hates maraschino cherries. "I've been interviewing at a lot of places. I interviewed at The Scruta last week. For a management position. That's why I saw the play there. Afterwards, I talked about my ideas for helping to manage the place, and keeping business up, all that stuff. I've interviewed to be a substitute teacher at the elementary school. I interviewed to be an assistant at the nursing home down the road. I even interviewed at Butterflake, but they said they probably aren't going to be hiring for a while. Smith's was the only restaurant I interviewed at. Back then, I had no idea you were ever going to want to interview there! But I didn't want to stop you. Just because I interviewed there doesn't mean you can't have the right. Besides, I didn't really think I would end up working there. Thinking about it now – it would be better for you. There really aren't many jobs for teenagers right now. It's hard these days, with the economy, finding jobs where you don't need a degree."

"But you got your degree in English, what good can that do you?"

Katie Mlinek

She shrugged. "There are higher chances of me getting a better job than your dad right now, because I at least *have* a degree. But neither of us are in that great a position."

I softened up a bit. She was right. I felt bad for taking so many digs at her. She's been working hard and I've been worried all about myself. "Are any of these jobs you would actually like?" I asked.

She shrugged again. "Probably. You can find a way to like anything if you try."

I nodded and looked down at my ice cream. "Like right now," she said, "eating at a Dairy Queen with you. I screwed up bad and I'm probably the worst mother in the world, but this ice cream is still delicious."

I laughed. "You're not the worst mom. Sorry for being a jerk and stuff."

And I was pretty sorry. I was partly to blame for holding all those cars up and I'm part of the reason why Mom's stressed about needing money and it's not like I've been a big help to either her or Dad.

"I'm sorry for not being very open with you. It wasn't right of me," she said.

"Does Dad know?" I asked.

"Some of it," she said. "But I'm trying to remain as calm as possible about everything. This has been hard on him. I think he feels like he's failed us. The company had been going down, and they fired all the top earning drivers before getting to him next. I think he wishes he had started looking for a job earlier, when he was worried about losing the trucking one. He's hit a lot of dead ends, looking for a new job."

I'm having a few too many surprises today. I had no idea Dad had been worried about losing his job, or that he's even been looking now. I only ever see him watching TV and crap. But I guess he *is* gone a lot, and I haven't even thought about where he's been. I remember, right when he lost his job, how he told me to stay in school and all that stuff, as if I'm in any danger of dropping out or something stupid like that. I swear, though, if I ever have a family someday, I'll have a degree and won't get anyone into this sort of mess. But maybe these surprises are good, even though they're about bad things. At least stuff is making more sense to me now.

"Whatever. Dad was never meant to be a trucker," I said. He really wasn't. He doesn't look like one. He doesn't wear flannel shirts or have a beard or sweat stains on all of his clothes. He does love crappy diner food, though. Mom says it's his kryptonite because he gets horrible heart burn over it but he loves it anyways. Instead of his truck bed being littered with gas station soda cups and cigarette butts, there are empty Tums containers.

"He liked trucking, though. He thinks there's something poetic about empty highways at night," Mom said.

"Yeah, I bet all his other trucker buddies were thinking the same thing."

Mom laughed. "Probably not. He liked them, though. He really did."

What a rollercoaster of emotions today. I hate it. I could feel my face starting to heat up, just the thought of some beer-gutted bums sitting in a trailer office and crossing his name off a list with a big fat red marker. I could see the secretary come in with long, fake orange fingernails and heavy mascara and a slight limp since she can't walk in heels right. She'd pick up the pile of papers and look at them and say in a New York accent, "ya wanna get rid-a Watta-worth? Good choice, Jimmy. That guy was no good, I tol' ya from the day he stahted here." I mean, he really didn't deserve it. Even if he's sort of falling apart now. He didn't deserve it.

Katie Mlinek

"Your father would never really say any of this stuff out loud, you know," Mom said. "As frustrating as he is right now, I think he's got it tougher than we realize."

I had never heard Mom talk like this before. But I liked being let in on these "adult" secrets. She never really talked to me about Dad's job, let alone her real thoughts on what was going on.

"We should get milkshakes more often," I said.

"I'm never getting a milkshake again," Mom said. "From now on, it's brownie sundaes for me. That was delicious."

"Yeah, well –"

Mom punched my shoulder. "Punch buggy, no punch backs!" she yelled. I looked at the road just in time to see a bright yellow punch buggy go around a corner.

"You punch like a girl," I said.

"Well, I *am* a girl," Mom said. "Sorry, I hope I didn't hurt you."

"You're good," I said. Actually, it really hurt. I imagined it already turning black and blue underneath my sleeve.

"You've got ice cream all over your mouth," Mom said, giggling and handing me a napkin. "I haven't seen you this messy since you were a baby and I had to feed you mushy peas on a spoon. Oh, and hey: don't tell Dad about the milkshake."

"Deal."

I took the napkin and wiped my mouth. Even Mom talking about me being a stupid baby and all was alright by me. I guess the here and now isn't as bad as I thought it was. The random Dairy Queen, the clouds that looked like they were straight from a Pixar movie, even the little, yellow punch buggy. Life isn't so

Comic Sans

bad, you know? Okay, well, it's not *great*, but that doesn't make it bad.

Katie Mlinek

Chapter 24

When Mom and I walked in through the doors, Dad was already home. He turned around and gave us a big smile.

"How was it?" Mom asked, setting her purse down.

"It was great. Everyone's still kicking around. Greg was even there."

Mr. Greg is an old friend of Dad's. He used to be a trucker, too, until he settled down with a family and started managing a Wendy's, but he and Dad still kept up with each other. They have a son, Lucas, who's just a year younger than me, and we used to go over there a lot and play "pirates". They don't live *that* far away, maybe like thirty minutes, but around here that's considered far away. As I got older, Dad and Mom would let me stay home alone when they went to visit them, so I haven't been in a couple of years. Even though it's boring now, I loved being home alone back then. They would let me rent a Blockbuster movie and Mom would make me popcorn before they left. Once I ate cereal before going to bed because I thought it was hilarious – you know, eating cereal *before* going to sleep instead of after waking up. Whatever. I was twelve.

"How's he doing?" Mom asked.

"Good. Real good. His two little boys are something else, from what I hear. And Lucas is doing well," Dad said, turning to me. "Plays a lot of sports."

I nodded, not super interested. Lucas was one of those kids who you could always play a game with and be happy, but just because he would do whatever you wanted to do. Lucas wasn't the sort of person you could really be close friends with. Like, you wouldn't ever tell him your most embarrassing stories or anything. Though we always had a good time playing.

"How was the interview?" Dad asked.

"Oh." I looked down. I didn't really know what to say. "I don't know. It was an interview." I shrugged. Mom wasn't making eye contact with me. She was pretending to dig through her purse for something.

"Ah well," Dad said. "Hey, that reminds me. Greg's minivan is acting up and he was wondering if I could stop over and help him out tonight. I said I would," Dad said.

"Oh? Okay," Mom said, looking up from her purse to smile. "Do you want to eat first?"

"We had some food while we were out. The guys paid. And Greg went back home real quick to get everything out and I said I'd run by here to let you know what was going on, see if there's anything you need while I'm out," Dad said.

Mom gave him a kiss. "Nope. Thanks for coming back here. Tell Deborah and the kids I said hi."

"Sure thing. James, I think you should come. You're about old enough that I start teaching you this stuff."

I nodded. "Sure. Let me go get changed first."

I ran back upstairs and laid my suit on my bed. I switched back to my more comfortable preference: a T-shirt and jeans. As I came back down the stairs I could hear Mom talking.

"I just don't know what to do," she said. "I mean, I don't know what changes to make. What am I doing wrong?"

I stopped on the stairs for a moment, worried that I was about to interrupt a serious conversation. There's nothing worse than coming into a room while your parents are having a secret, private conversation (in the *kitchen*, the least private place in the world) and they stop talking and just watch you as you get yourself a glass of water or banana or something like that.

"I'm 165 pounds," Mom said as I came into the kitchen. "Do you know how much butter my weight amounts to? I really just don't know how I gained it all."

It was weird to hear Mom talking about something as casual as weight, especially after the intense talk she and I just had.

"Don't worry," Dad said. He was sitting at the table with his car keys in hand. "For a woman your age and everything, I'm sure it's normal. Besides, muscle weighs more than fat. With all the running around you do all day, I'm sure you've got a lot of muscle." They both turned to me. "Well there you are, James. Ready to go?"

"Yup." Mom gave me a hug goodbye and I let her.

Dad and I got in the car. I remember the last time I was at Mr. Greg's house, maybe six years ago, they made homemade spaghetti sauce but I thought it was disgusting because I'd only ever had the store-bought kind, so I threw up their dinner all over the table. It was awful. I remember how much Mom and Dad lectured me on the drive home about being polite and not puking on special chinaware and everything. Now I felt all embarrassed about having to return to the scene of that horrible crime.

Comic Sans

Dad and I sat in silence while he drove for a while. I kept running over the day in my head. What are Eleanor and her family doing now? Are they talking about me, right this second? Forbidding her from ever seeing a psycho like me again? After such a helter skelter day, I was feeling pretty tired. And the thought of how much I just screwed up everything with Eleanor made me even more exhausted.

"I've got good news," Dad said, taking his eyes off the road for a moment to grin at me. "Want to hear it? But you can't tell Mom. I'm saving it for our anniversary."

"Go for it," I said.

"The guys have a lead on a job for me," Dad said, glancing at me to see my reaction. "That's why I met up with them today. They still hear all the industry stuff that I don't have much of an in on anymore. There's a company starting up nearby that's all about fresh fruit. That's it. It'll be fancy, exotic fruit, but the point is that it's as fresh as possible. Which means I'd be doing quick spurts of driving, no more leaving for weeks and weeks to go to far places. I'd just be transporting stuff from the seaport an hour away back to the store. I think I could really get the job," Dad said.

"Oh my gosh. Really?" I asked, sitting up.

Dad nodded. "But *don't tell Mom*. I really want to surprise her."

Geez, my parents are the most exhausting people ever. All this "don't tell him that," and "keep this a secret from her," and then they get all mad at each other because they won't tell each other everything. From now on, I'll tell everyone everything just to keep life easier. Well, okay, not *everything*. People don't need to hear if I'm feeling gassy or gross stuff like that.

"I don't see why you should wait," I said. "She'd probably feel less stressed if she knew now."

Katie Mlinek

"Yeah, but if this falls through, which could happen early on, she'd be even more stressed. My buddy Jackson knows a guy in the company and is putting in a good word for me. I'm going to wait to see how that goes, and then I could get an interview and snag the job from there."

I shrugged. "If that's what you think is best."

"That *is* what I think is best," Dad said, laughing a bit. "You aren't stressed, too, are you?"

I shook my head with another shrug. Dad kept taking his eyes away from the road to look at me.

"Well, hey," he said. "I'm going to pull through for us. I'm going to get this job."

I nodded. "I know."

We pulled up to Mr. Greg's house, which was quaint and small and everything suburban.

"Aww, thanks for getting here on such short notice, David, it's really great of you," Mr. Greg said as he opened the door. In fact, I think he started talking before he even touched the doorknob. Hearing his familiar Canadian accent made me feel like a little kid again. "You know, I'm really blessed to have a friend like you. That's what I was telling Deborah right before getting the door just now. Yup, I sure am blessed. Is this James? Boy, have you grown!"

"We got here as soon as we could," Dad said, shaking his hand.

I hate when people talk about how much I've grown right in front of me. I don't even care what people are saying, if they're talking *about* me (or as Mr. Greg would say, "aboot") while I'm right there without actually talking *to* me, then it's a problem in my book. And that wasn't even my first mark against Mr. Greg.

Comic Sans

The first thing I noticed when he opened the door was his neon orange Hawaiian shirt and blue plaid pants. This guy was something else. For some reason, I don't remember any of this stuff from the last time I was here as a kid. The cheesy clothes or anything.

Mr. Greg opened the door wider and invited us inside. The coffee table in the middle of the room had foam duct-taped around each of the corners.

"So how's the family?" Dad asked.

"Well, Deborah's got our fourth one on the way," he said, leading us into the kitchen where Ms. Deborah stood with what looked like an exercise ball for a stomach. Her hair was in a ponytail that had half-fallen out and the sink was littered with pots and pans. She was mixing something together in a giant bowl, but, as crazy as the place was, that kitchen smelled better than anything I've ever smelled in my entire life.

"Well David, you just look terrific, eh!" Deborah squealed in the same Canadian accent, setting down the mixing bowl and coming to give him a hug.

"Speak for yourself, Deborah! Congratulations to the both of you," Dad said. "When's the due date?"

"Oh, *aboot* a month from now," Mr. Greg said. Two kids ran through the kitchen in just their underwear. I realized they were the babies last I had been here.

"You two! Get something decent to wear! Up the stairs now, come on," Ms. Deborah called, waddling after the kids.

"Yup, life sure has been hectic, but we love it," Mr. Greg said, leading us to the back of the house. "It's really great. Really, really great." He shook his head. "Well! You gotta stop me from all my yammering. It's not often I get to see old buddies anymore,

Katie Mlinek

and today was so nice. But I didn't get much of a chance to talk with just you. What's new with you, eh?"

"Oh, not much else," Dad said. "James here is in his junior year of high school. It's true what they say, time flies."

"Oh, goodness! You've got a man on your hands here, David," Mr. Greg said, winking at me. He opened up the tool shed and started pulling out everything he had. "So I don't fully know what's wrong with the car, though I'm worried it has something to do with the transmission. And I've got the car up on a jack right over here."

"This is great, thank you," Dad said.

We went over to the car port, where a white Dodge Grand Caravan was sitting under the quickly setting sun. Dad set to work immediately, asking me to hand him different tools and such. He did all of the work, and I just watched. He explained different parts of the car, the tools I should use to fix each part, what not to do, what problems to look for, a load of stuff I would probably never remember.

"This one is a real humdoozer, that's for sure," Greg began. "It's starting to get to be too small for us anyways. I don't know why I don't just get a new car, seeing as we have to find room for a baby carrier now. And those things get bigger and more expensive by the day. Deborah and I were looking around at flea markets for a new one until we realized that car seats could expire. Who knew? I mean, since when were car seats like milk, eh? I really just don't understand it. I'm telling you, this world is structured to strip us of our hard-earned money in every single way, *doncha know.*"

"How's Lucas doing?" Dad asked, getting up from under the car.

Comic Sans

"He's at weight training practice right now. He's a fine boy, he really is. Does sports year round. Football is his favorite, when fall comes around."

This surprised me. Lucas was a pretty skimpy kid, last I saw. Whenever we dressed up for "pirates," his costumes never fit me. It was hard to imagine him as a football player now. His blonde hair probably got even brighter and I bet all the cheerleaders go crazy over him. It was making me sick to my stomach. I wished I could see him again suddenly. Just to make sure he's still innocent and fun and stuff like when we were kids. I stopped wanting to go to their house because Lucas got boring. He just wanted to play video games all the time, never "pirates" or "dragons" or "save the kingdom." I was the one who invented that last game. I missed them all, though.

"That's great! What do you think you'll name the baby?" Dad asked.

"Well now, I've always thought Andrew was a fantastic name, and it's one I hope to use, either as a first or middle name. Of course, Deborah is partial to David, like her father, though it would be strange to have a kid accidentally named after you. I like classic names. Arthur is a great name, I love all the Rs in it. Now, this all does depend on the gender. Seeing as I have all boys, it's strange to think of having a girl now. Though I'd be fine with that. I'd really love it. I don't care either way."

It was about then that I realized Mr. Greg would never stop talking. He was like a bag of chips. Once you eat one chip, you have to eat them all, and you just feel greasy and oily and awful afterwards. I was starting to feel gross after only twenty minutes of Mr. Greg talking at Dad nonstop. Dad was a seasoned pro, though. He mixed in enough "mmhmms" and "of courses" to seem engaged, all while working on the car engine.

This must be what having a large family does to you. Mr. Greg was acting as if he hadn't seen another civilized person in

Katie Mlinek

months, even though he had just been at a bar. Running around in underwear probably seemed normal to him.

"Alright," Dad said while Mr. Greg took a breath in the middle of his story about five o'clock traffic on Thursdays. "Why don't you turn the car on and let's see how this baby runs!"

Mr. Greg hopped in the car, put the keys in, and turned on the engine. I've never understood why people say engines "purr," because really at their best they're more of a polar bear growl. So anyways, it growled and they cheered and I wiped the grease from my hands onto my jeans.

"Thank you so much, David," he said, getting out to shake his hand. "That was quite the feat, especially as last minute as this. Here." He fished out his wallet and pulled out a fifty-dollar bill. "Take this."

"Absolutely not." Dad waved his hands and backed away. Here we go. Now I get to stand through a twenty minute "politeness" argument. I could envision Mr. Greg and Ms. Deborah now, having daily standoffs outside the kitchen door, each one urging each other to be the first to cross the barrier. I hate "politeness" arguments. Makes everything a heck of a lot slower than it needs to be. I sort of wanted him to take it, though. Fifty dollars can be dinner, gas, that part Dad needs to fix *our* car.

"Really, you saved me thousands of dollars," Mr. Greg said. "Mechanics are just so expensive these days, they really are. This is nothing I'm giving you, you really deserve more."

They continued back and forth like that until Dad pointed out how fast the sun was setting, and that we should probably go inside. He took the lead, and Mr. Greg hung back a little bit, waving me over to him.

"Take it," he said, trying to slip me the fifty, "and give it to your old man when the time is right. That's a good boy."

Comic Sans

I would have taken it if he hadn't added that little line right at the end there. I half expected him to pat me on the head like a dog. Maybe then it would have been acceptable for me to bark and bite him.

"Sorry, sir," I said. "It doesn't feel right to take your money. Thanks anyways, though."

Mr. Greg seemed to give up, and came inside with us. As great as the kitchen smelled when we came back in, I was glad to be leaving. We walked back through the living room and I saw Ms. Deborah sitting on the couch, reading to her two youngest kids. They were curled up against her on either side, and one was fast asleep. He had his little fist propped up right underneath his chin and furrowed eyebrows, as if he had fallen asleep deep in thought. Ms. Deborah was reading "If You Give a Mouse a Cookie" in a soft, quiet voice. That was my favorite book when I was little. And suddenly, all I wanted was to sit down like the two little kids and listen in. I wanted to curl up and smell the cinnamon and chocolate from the kitchen and feel the little window air conditioner cool the room and listen to "If You Give a Mouse a Cookie." I really did. I wanted to have a milk mustache, because when I was little and read that book, I always gave myself a milk mustache and then showed it to Mom. It was my favorite part of the book. And she'd laugh and get a little napkin to wipe it off and one time, she even let me have an actual cookie. I loved that book.

Ms. Deborah looked up at us and smiled, giving a little wave goodbye while still reading. She probably had it memorized. And as we said goodbye to Mr. Greg, I felt a little jealous that he got to go back inside and hear the end of the story.

Dad and I got back into our cold car and pulled out of the driveway.

Katie Mlinek

Chapter 25

The Monday after, I woke up with a vicious headache. It felt like three hundred rhinos knocking on my forehead. It felt like hell. So I got up and checked my temperature and it was like 102, which, judging by Mom's reaction when she saw the thermometer, is pretty bad.

There's nothing more stupid than being sick in spring. I mean, who gets a cold in spring? Biologically, it's unlikely, and it makes you feel like a complete wimp. It's warm and beautiful outside, and that means nature could never allow for germs, right? If you can't even be sick in a *normal* way, how can you ever expect to get by anything in life?

Being sick always sucks. But if it's winter then it's great, because you don't feel like you're missing out on anything. But when you're sick in *spring*, you spend all day looking out the window watching couples bike and little kids bring flowers to their moms and everyone being happy and jolly while you feel sorry for yourself.

Mom has never told either Dad or I her secret, but whenever either of us is sick, she does something to the medicine that makes it taste like mint instead of gross artificial grape or cherry or watermelon. So I've never had bad medicine in my entire life. She gave me some and told me to just rest and not worry about school or anything.

Comic Sans

After such a crappy weekend, it wasn't very comforting to start off with this stupid sickness. I treated myself to extra syrup on my Eggo waffles for breakfast, but then I puked it all up, so that didn't work out too well. Another symbol of all my failures, I guess. Right now, being overdramatic was the only thing keeping me going.

Maybe I'm just stress sick. I mean, between my loss of any hope at getting a job and embarrassing myself horribly in front of Eleanor and her mom, I'm perfectly fine with just staying home all day. I really don't want to see Eleanor right now. Hopefully my being gone will help her get distracted by other things and give her time to miss me or something. And time for me to digest all that car jargon Dad threw at me the other day.

I wish I had my phone at least, so I could talk to *someone*. But as I thought about it more, I realized there wasn't even anyone to talk to.

I started watching some game show, curled up on the couch with a blanket. The game shows stop airing at 11:00, which means I'll have to switch to watching a bunch of home improvement shows or something. Or maybe a nice documentary about deep sea fish. Really, anything other than sports. I hate sports. Most guys hate me for hating sports, but I don't even care. Sometimes I like to watch sports at the end of the game when all the football players take their helmets off and they have this crazy hair that goes everywhere. Some of them have hair that goes below their shoulders. Doesn't it get hot, all bunched up in their helmet all day long? I wonder how freeing it must feel to take it off, let the whole mangy mess just fall. I'm super curious about it, but not enough to actually grow my hair that long and try it. Besides, then I'd have to wear a man bun all the time and if there's anything I hate more than sports, it's anti-sports-man-bun-wearing people. I don't want to ally myself with that kind at all.

Katie Mlinek

The phone rang in the kitchen and I just let it keep going. I really didn't want to stand up. I felt so cozy with my blanket and unwashed pajamas and the familiar voice of the game show host. Besides, the woman on the show was about to decide whether or not she wanted what's behind Door Two, and I'm pretty convinced that the free boat is behind Door Three, and I really want to see her choose the wrong door.

Finally the phone stopped ringing and I heard Mom talking to someone in the kitchen. Normally I strain to listen to her conversations, but I wasn't interested today. I was just waiting for the silly commercial to be over so I could find out which door was concealing the free boat.

"Yes, I got there right as the interview ended," I heard Mom say. I sat up slightly to hear her better. Is she talking about me? Probably not, I was being silly, she could be talking about any of her number of interviews.

"Oh yes, I found him okay. Thank you very much for your help. Yes, of course. Okay now. Buh-bye."

Mom hung up the phone and came into the living room.

"Who was that?" I asked.

"Mrs. Iding from down the street," she said.

"What?" I sat up, but the throbbing in my head tried to beat me back down. "Why?"

"Sweetie, *sweetie*, lie back down. You've got to rest." Mom gave me a peck on my head. "She just wanted to know if I had found you okay after your interview the other day. When she called to let me know you were there."

"Why didn't she call two days ago?" I asked.

Comic Sans

Mom shrugged. The game show was over, the woman had won her free boat, and the only thing behind Door Three was a pile of trash. Guess it's a good thing I wasn't there.

"I'm going to go. There's soup in the fridge, just warm it up in the microwave. Don't try to do anything else today, okay? Ignore the mess in the kitchen and everything. Your Dad and I will get home later today. I think we're going to go for a nice walk somewhere later on. I hope you feel better." And with that, Mom left, leaving me in peace to watch the last game show of the day.

I can never tell when she says stuff like "ignore the mess in the kitchen" if she secretly wants me to actually pay attention to it and clean it up or if she's just saying it because it's on her mind. And her and Dad going for a walk…? It seems so weird. They're not big outdoorsy people or anything. I don't know if they've walked for *fun* since that one time Dad was gone for a whole month on a big haul to Mexico. He came back with an "authentic" maraca for me that I now think he must have gotten at some gas station down there, and fancy spicy chocolate for Mom. And they decided we should all go for a nice two hour "walk" at some park we had to *drive* to so we could catch up and be a family again and stuff. I was maybe five or so, and I remember I was starting to get too big for my shoes and they squeezed real bad and now I associate the word "walk" with torture. But still, Mom and Dad planning to just casually taking a walk together on a Monday night?

Oh. Today's their anniversary.

Katie Mlinek

Chapter 26

I stayed in the same place on the couch for almost the entire day. I guess I was sick with the flu or something and Mom's medicine didn't seem to be working. I just didn't want to get up. I watched so many houses be renovated that I started to feel like ours was the only house in America that wasn't fixed up.

And how do so many people have an extra couple million dollars to waste on beach condos? There's obviously enough of them to fill up a full seven seasons of these shows. So much for helping out all the rest of us poor people in this world – what they need is a *private pool* right next to the beach. I hate these people, all the sniveling wives who won't budge on anything they want and their good-for-nothing husbands who got rich by chance. But it makes me feel better to hate them. It's just so easy.

I don't even know what I spent the whole day doing. It's weird how days feel so long when you're at school and over in a blip when you're at home. I puked a lot, and my nose was constantly stinging something terrible. I found Oreos in the pantry, ate a bunch of those, then puked all that up, too. I was really craving cookies and milk, though. Or at the very least, chocolate cereal. I don't know why. I puked everything up.

I kept running to the upstairs bathroom to puke since the downstairs one was broken. But in the afternoon, I didn't make it. I had to run into the bathroom across from the kitchen and man,

Comic Sans

I didn't even have guts to spill, it was all just stomach acid burning up my throat. I felt terrible. Mom would be so upset if she saw that I had puked in a toilet that couldn't flush. But then I remembered that Dad had gotten it fixed not that long ago and felt silly for getting all worked up about it. I had completely forgotten that he did that.

When I came back to the kitchen, Mom was home and putting groceries away. She immediately came over to me and put her hand on my forehead.

"Oh, James, you're burning up," she said.

"Did you get Cocoa Crunch?" I asked.

She took her hand off my forehead. "What?"

"You know, that awesome chocolate cereal stuff."

Mom laughed a little and went back to putting away groceries. "No, sweetie, those chocolate cereals are overpriced and *terrible* for you. The last thing you need right now is bowls full of sugar."

She was putting away another pack of Oreos and I immediately reached for it.

"You know, we should help out the neighborhood more." She sighed and looked out the window. "Apparently everyone's trying to get together to make a community garden near those big, expensive houses that aren't selling well."

"Uh-huh," I said, not paying any attention.

I tried to grab an Oreo but Mom slapped at my hand. "Absolutely not! Back onto the couch and under the covers. No cookies for you. You need rest."

I silently obeyed Mom and went back into the living room. Luckily for me, Mythbusters was marathoning, and all the hours

Katie Mlinek

of explosions and cheesy jokes and science terms soon blurred together. I think at some point Dad got home and he and Mom left to go on their walk but I hardly registered anything.

Once it got to be around dinner time (or at least it started getting darker outside, I don't know what time it was), I figured I might as well eat a banana or something. I was starting to feel better. As in I was starting to feel human again. So I got up and went into the kitchen and there was Mom and Dad, sitting at our little rickety table with a candle between them and a bowl of Kraft mac-n-cheese.

"Hey, James, are you getting hungry for dinner?" Mom said, starting to stand up.

"No no no, it's okay, sit back down," I said. "I'm just going to grab something real quick." I grabbed a banana off of the counter and started to leave so that Mom and Dad could keep having their little macaroni dinner together.

"I can get you some mac-n-cheese real quick," Mom said.

"She breaded it on top, too, so it's fancy," Dad said.

"It's okay, I'm not that hungry. Thanks, though," I said. I left the kitchen and started walking upstairs.

"James?" Mom called. "I want you to check your temperature again. You still look a little pale."

"Okay, Mom!" I shouted back. I went upstairs and pulled out the thermometer. 99.3. Dangit. Guess I do still have something of a fever. But I didn't want Mom to know because she'd stop eating her dinner and make me that special secret medicine and then Dad would blow out the candle and they'd just go to bed early and all like they always do. So I just went to sleep, piling on blankets in the hopes of breaking my fever.

Comic Sans

Chapter 27

Probably the weirdest thing about my school, other than the triangle windows in the lunchroom, is the walls. There are giant corkboards colored like Dijon mustard that take up most of the space, and on either side is where the lockers are smashed together. Normally the corkboards are empty, save for a few "Save the Rainforest!" petitions and reminders of the National Honor Society car washes. But now, since the elections for class president are coming up and all, the corkboards are jammed full of neon posters from Office Depot.

I noticed Eleanor underneath one of the corkboards, surrounded by posters and staples and her way-too-big bookbag. Suddenly I felt terrible. With everything that had been happening, I completely forgot about her running for president, and how hard she must have been working all this time. Maybe she was working when I biked to her house last Friday, and I interrupted her in the middle of something and set her back and all. Gosh, I feel awful.

"Hey ,Eleanor, how's it going?" I asked.

She stapled another poster to the wall. "All I've had to eat today was a spoonful of Nutella. That's how it's going. Can you hand me that poster right there?"

"How many posters are you going to put on just one wall?" I asked, picking the poster up.

"Only two. Hey." She set down the poster and looked at me. "Are you okay? Why weren't you in school yesterday? I'm so sorry, I've just been stressed and stuff and I forgot for a moment, but seriously, are you okay? We were all worried about you. The group, I mean. You *never* miss anything."

I smiled. It's nice knowing that she was worried about me missing school and everything. But I felt another pang of guilt that I had forgotten *everything*: the group project, the class president elections – and she's leaving for the whole summer! How could I have forgotten all this?

"Yeah, I was just sick. How was yesterday?"

"Fine. I mean, we hardly got anything done. Mason had a weird…I don't know, temper tantrum thing? He just got mad over nothing and stormed out of class. Then he came back at the end as if nothing had happened." Eleanor picked up the poster again and started positioning it against the wall.

"Woah. That's really weird," I said. "Here, let me help."

The poster was purple – no surprise there, everything she has is purple – and it said, "This isn't a joke! Vote for Eleanor Iding!" Her picture was in between the two sentences, but the most beautiful thing about it was that in it, she was wearing the clown nose I had given her earlier in the year.

"Wow!" I said. "I can't believe this! I can't believe you kept this!"

She giggled. "Thought you might like it. And isn't the font perfect for it?"

Comic Sans

"Yeah," I said, though I wouldn't know.

She started hanging it up on the wall, and I automatically grabbed the poster and held it in place so that she only had to staple it.

"How many more do you have to do?" I asked.

"Only those three," she said, pointing to the last ones on the floor and glancing behind her. "Oh my gosh. Look at that poster. I can't believe this is my competition."

Across the hallway, there was a poster so doused in glitter that a small pile of gold sparkles had fallen to the floor right beneath it. It belonged to Alicia Stai, who's just now become the official worst person on this *planet*.

For one, she's single-handedly created some of the worst social constructs in this school just because she wanted to. See, once a girl has a boyfriend, she's automatically entered into the exclusive Slut Club. I'm not the one who came up with that name, I swear. That's just what everyone at school calls it. It's a group of girls who all have boyfriends. That's all it is. But they all go on double and triple and quadruple dates together, and tell each other which lipstick looks best on their boyfriend's cheeks, and constantly post pictures on social media about how much they love their boyfriend. It makes me really sick. They all hang out around Alicia Stai's locker, because she *always* has a boyfriend, and whenever they find out someone just got in a relationship, they hunt her down and do their best to drag her in. Some girls are able to stay clear. Most get pulled in. And those relationships last maybe like three weeks, tops. Anything more than that is short of a miracle.

"This is good news," I said, unable to tear my eyes away from the trainwreck of a poster. "This hardly counts as competition." I walked across the hall and put a finger on the poster. Gluey glitter

Katie Mlinek

came off on my finger and I rubbed it on my pants, but then the glitter stuck all to it.

"Now you're like a walking advertisement," Eleanor said, laughing.

Just then, the bell rang for first period. I helped Eleanor gather up all of her posters and walked with her down the hallway.

"Want me to help you finish stapling these during lunch?" I asked.

"Sure, I'll be on the third floor," she said. "Just these last few posters and then I'm done." I gave her a salute as goodbye and walked off.

When lunchtime came around, I was on the third floor before she got there. Already, so much space on the corkboards were taken up by campaign posters, since the elections for every grade happen at the same time. It's poor scheduling, but that's mostly because no one really bothered trying to schedule anything at all. I don't know who's in charge of this kind of stuff. The people in charge of things never even seem to understand what it is they're really in charge of. If *I* ran this school, things would be lot different. First, no red lines in the hallway. Unnecessary restrictions like that can go flying out the triangle windows, which brings me to my next change: no triangle windows. They barely let in any light. And if I was in charge, lunches would be free, and you could choose your groups in every class, and the A/C would actually work in this forsaken building. And I would make sure that Eleanor got to be president.

Eleanor came running up the stairs, posters and staples practically falling out of her hands.

Comic Sans

"Sorry, sorry, sorry," she said, still heaving from her run. "I had to talk to a teacher. Have you been waiting here long? I'm so sorry!"

"It's okay, no worries. Here, I'll take those." I took the posters from her. "Where do you want to hang these up?" I was feeling all jittery inside now that she was here. The light from outside was hitting her in a way that made her normally dark hair look like strands of gold, and she had a little bit of sweat on the top of her forehead, but part of me really wanted to kiss her. Right there and then. I don't know what came over me, I really don't. But what if I still had germs from being sick and everything, and just being near her got *her* sick? I'd feel awful. I'd never come to school again so I never even have the *chance* of getting someone sick.

I followed Eleanor to where she wanted to put the next poster, and held it up while she stapled it. She had to stand really close to me to punch all the staples in. This poster had little paper figure things, all handmade, holding hands at the bottom of the poster. They were each decorated with tiny, intricate details, like small beads for earrings, string sewn on for hair, even little ties cut out of fabric.

"Woah, Ellie, did you make all these…what are these?" I asked.

"Paper dolls," she said. "I was cleaning up my room the other day and found a paper doll kit I used to have as a kid. I made tons of paper dolls and played with them all the time, until my little sister ripped most of them. And I don't know, seeing them just made me sort of want to make more. For old time's sake."

"That's so funny, I found something in my room the other day, too!" I said. "It was a little old soccer ball I used to love." And as I said it, I immediately felt stupid. I really don't know why my brain is in such a fuzz that I can't say normal, interesting things. "I

Katie Mlinek

mean, it reminded me of when I was a kid and all, too." I stopped talking. Eleanor looked at me and nodded. I couldn't tell what the nod really meant. Nodding in a "what a fascinating tidbit about your childhood" kind of way, or nodding in a "why am I still talking to this loser?" kind of way?

After she finished stapling the poster, we moved on to the next giant corkboard.

"Hey, when is the English project due again?" I asked, just to get conversation rolling again.

"We have one more week," Eleanor said. I knew perfectly well that we had only one more week, but it's okay. We've got mostly everything done, which amazes even me. As I thought about it – and I can't believe I'm saying this, I really can't – I realized I'm going to miss this project, and the group. But maybe, if I can get my phone back sort of soon, I can join the group chat again and we'll all stay friends over the summer. Even Mason, if he's not getting mad all the time, whatever that was about. And Miranda will probably give us virtual hugs, and Veronica will always have the perfect amount of sass, and Eleanor can try to teach me how to juggle over text. It could work out. I really think it could.

Comic Sans

Chapter 28

Eleanor and I walked into English class and someone had lined up three chairs and was stretched out, sleeping their life away. Despite that person, everyone else was having a party. I mean, a *party*. A group of kids were gathered around a computer watching YouTube videos, people had pulled out Cards Against Humanity in the corner of the room, and another group was busting dance moves to some pop song. I looked to the front of the room and there was a substitute, zombie-eyed and scrolling through Facebook on Mrs. Desarrollee's computer.

"Well," I said to Eleanor, "this will be an interesting class."

I set down my stuff and looked around the room for our group. That's when I saw Miranda and Veronica huddled together on the floor, practically underneath a desk like they were ducking from a nuclear bomb. Eleanor and I flashed each other a concerned look and went over.

"Um…what's going on?" I asked. "I didn't know this was the new meeting place."

Miranda looked up at me and I saw tears just beginning to trickle down her face. Veronica had buried her head in her knees. Oh geez. Someone get me out of here. Now.

Eleanor immediately crouched down and put her hand around Veronica. "What's wrong?" she asked, rubbing her back.

"Her boyfriend broke up with her," Miranda said.

I groaned. I didn't even know she had a boyfriend. I could really use one of those jet packs right about now – just zoom out the window and let these girls work out their melodrama on their own. But it's too late, I'm here, and leaving will make me seem like the biggest jerk in the world. So I sat down next to Eleanor and braced myself for even more tears.

"What happened?" Eleanor asked. I could hear a sob coming from somewhere between Veronica's hair and jeans, and she started to shake.

"He broke up with her in front of everyone." Miranda was still crying. "*Everyone,*" she whispered.

"Why are *you* crying?" I asked her.

"I don't know." Miranda looked away. "It's just so sad."

I used all of my internal strength to stop myself from rolling my eyes. Though I suppose that would have been a good way to honor Veronica.

Veronica lifted her head and let out a big sigh. She kept rubbing her eyes, her forehead, the bridge of her nose. She started nodding.

"It's going to be okay," she said, choking on her words slightly.

"You're right," Eleanor said, still rubbing her back. "It *is* going to be okay. Do you want to talk about what happened?"

"I don't know." Veronica seemed in danger of crying again. "Well, I guess I do. Sort of. He just started, I don't know, getting more distant? Like he didn't care about me anymore. I didn't know what was going on. I've been worried for a while, but I didn't want to push anything, you know? So I just sort of let him be. If he wasn't going to talk to me, I wasn't going to talk to him.

Comic Sans

But I was going *crazy* inside, like really crazy. And then today he stood up in the middle of Biology and said to me, 'I'm done.' And I said, 'No you're not, you haven't done number fifteen yet.' I thought he was talking about our paper. And he said, 'No, I'm done with *you*.' And everyone heard and watched him go up to the teacher and ask for a bathroom pass. And then he just…left the room."

"Oh, Veronica. That's awful. I'm so sorry."

"Yeah." Veronica's face scrunched up again and she started to cry. Her voice broke up like a radio with poor signal. "I just don't know where…where it went wrong."

"Well, James is a guy, ask him," Miranda said. Everyone looked at me. I shrugged.

"I don't…I wouldn't…what? I don't know this stuff." Is it just me, or was the A/C working even worse than normal today?

"What can we do to help?" Eleanor asked, still using her soft voice.

Veronica shook her head. "Nothing. Nothing."

We sat around helpless for a little bit, Eleanor rubbing Veronica's back like her life depended on it, Miranda having her own little pity-party, and me looking at the ceiling as if I'd never seen it before. But then I started thinking, you know, about how at first Veronica seems like the sort of person who would be all over the Slut Club. But she's really not. She was very quiet about this whole boyfriend thing, especially if I didn't even know she had one, unlike most other girls who like to talk about their boyfriend just so everyone knows they have one. You know, Veronica's cooler than most people give her credit for. It's probably my fault for not having noticed her mention this guy at all.

Katie Mlinek

Veronica was still crying pretty steadily into her knees. It was so weird, seeing her emotionally vulnerable like this. She's like an Exact-O knife. She doesn't look intimidating or anything, but she's got a sharp edge to her. This was all too weird for me – no cunning comebacks, no angsty groans, just a sad teenage girl sitting on the floor while everyone else parties.

"What's going on?" We all looked up and there was Mason, standing over everyone with his arms crossed. Miranda and Eleanor looked at each other hesitantly, probably worried he was going to lose his temper over nothing again. Everyone tensed up. Geez. This place is exhausting. Why can't everyone just calm down a little? Eat chocolate or whatever? I really don't know what to do here.

"Veronica's boyfriend broke up with her," Miranda said.

"Then why are *you* crying?" he asked her, sitting down. I laughed a little.

"I asked the same thing," I said.

"Men have no hearts," Miranda said, getting a little red in the face.

"Hey. Chill out," Mason said. He tapped Veronica, who had buried her head in her knees again. "So Nathan broke up with you? Why don't you come out of that shell, huh, are you a turtle or something?"

"Be easy on her," Eleanor said, raising a threatening eyebrow.

Mason raised his hands in defense. "I *am*. Veronica. Listen. Look at me."

Veronica raised her head and looked at Mason. Her face was all blotchy and she had black stuff rubbed all under her eyes.

"Hey, there you are. Well. You're looking tough."

Comic Sans

Veronica just looked at him with her streaked face.

Mason took a breath. "Well, I don't know what happened," he said. "But I do know that he doesn't matter. Okay? That much is clear. That much you know, right? Anyone who can make you this upset doesn't matter. Seriously. Any guy who would hurt you like this is an asshole, and can go to hell. I'll personally escort him there."

"But she loved him!" Miranda said.

"God, Miranda, we're *sixteen*, no one really loves anyone. No one's getting *married* anytime soon."

Veronica gave Mason a small smile. She wiped her tears away again. "You're right," she said, laughing a little. "He was kind of an asshole."

"Exactly. He looks like one, too."

Veronica laughed again. "Well, he had nice hair," she said.

"No! It looked like poop on top of his asshole face! Veronica, that guy was no good. Do him a favor, show him how much better you are than him. Don't cry a ton or lose your mind or anything. Show him you're way better without him and maybe he'll learn a lesson."

Everyone was laughing and Veronica was laughing and Miranda wasn't crying anymore. Eleanor took her arm off and Veronica stretched out a little and we all stood up.

"I really love you guys," Veronica said. "I know this is stupid, this project and everything. I didn't think I'd make friends out of it. But you guys are great. God, this is cheesy."

We all laughed again and started talking at once, how much we all care about her too and stuff like that. I mean, we weren't singing *Kumbaya* or holding hands or anything like that. We all just looked at each other and felt, well, very much *together*. I had

Katie Mlinek

sort of forgotten how much the rest of the class was partying, to tell you the truth. It was just us in our little corner, Mason and Veronica and Miranda and Eleanor and I as a group, a real group. Not a cliché clique or exclusive club. Just a group of friends. You know, I guess crying can lead to good things sometimes, too.

Comic Sans

Chapter 29

Mom was so happy that it scared me. I mean, for real. When I came home, she had vacuumed the living room and dusted around the TV and the whole kitchen was practically spotless and she was singing an old doo-wop song that I didn't know the name of.

"Hey," I said hesitantly, slinging my bookbag into a chair.

"Don't put that there," she said, breaking her song. "I just scrubbed down all the chairs."

"What? Why do you have to scrub chairs?"

"Chairs get dirty," Mom said simply. She gave me a hug. "How was school, sweetie?"

"Fine. What's for dinner?"

"Your father's making spaghetti and meatballs!" Mom said in a sing-songy voice. "Did you know, when we were dating, he used to make me spaghetti and meatballs every Monday night? Because I hated Mondays. I had a class with a professor that I hated. He was *horrible*, he used to give us assignments that were really cruel if he was in a bad mood, which he always was. He used to make us explain the grammatical purpose of every word in a chapter of *Moby Dick*, stuff like that. But sorry, that isn't the point. I just really hated him. But like I was saying, your father started this tradition, this Monday-night-spaghetti-and-meatball tradition, so I would always have something to look forward to that day, and we kept it up for a long time. Till I got pregnant with you, and I just never felt like eating tomato sauce anymore."

"Sorry I ruined that for you," I said, laughing. I kind of liked this, Mom being in a good mood and all. I had no idea why she was, though.

"So you're feeling definitely better?" she said, resting her hand on my forehead briefly. "You look better!"

"Yeah, just fine," I said.

"Good. I'm glad it wasn't anything serious. Without health insurance, well, you know."

"Oh."

"Well, we could have used your remains as compost for the community garden," Mom said.

I started cracking up. "Mom! Hey!"

Just then, Dad came through the door and Mom went straight to him to give him a kiss. Now this was *really* unusual. I can't even count how many times Dad has come home to Mom asleep on the couch in her hair curlers, some infomercial still playing on the TV, whenever she tried to stay up late waiting for him to come home. I looked away as Mom and Dad kissed – it's just so *gross* – and then Mom even let Dad sit on one of the cleaned chairs.

"How'd the interview go?" Mom asked.

Ah, I remember now. Dad had said he was going to tell her about the job opportunity on their anniversary. He must have, and now she's super happy. Hence, clean house. Dots connected. Boom.

Comic Sans

Dad smiled and rubbed his hair. "Really great. I liked the guy a lot, and I'm pretty sure he liked me, too. Real down-to-earth-type, you know? And the job has great benefits."

"I'm so glad," Mom said, giving him one of the biggest, realest smiles I've seen in a long time. "I thought we should celebrate! Look what I got today."

Mom grabbed a bottle of wine from the pantry and put it proudly on the table.

"Methode Carbonique Pinot Noir?" Dad said, wide-eyed, looking the bottle over, holding it up to the light. "Honey! You didn't have to do this. I can hardly even pronounce it."

Mom laughed and shrugged. "We needed to do something! This is the best news we've had in ages. James, go turn the radio on! Put it on 76.1. "

I got up and turned on the radio. It was some old classic rock station, and the radio must have been turned up real loud the last time it was played because the whole house started shaking.

"C'mon, let's get some spaghetti and meatballs going!" Mom yelled. I saw Dad laugh, but his voice was drowned out by the music. Mom started boiling the noodles and Dad started getting the meatball sauce together and I sat at the newly cleaned table doing homework. But I didn't mind it. Mom and Dad laughed and talked together, though I couldn't hear what they were saying well with the music playing so loudly. But there's something about loud music that, I don't know, makes everything feel in tune, with the same vibrations going through every plate and cup and bloodstream and squeaky clean chair. And we were all in the same room, feeling all the same beats even as we did different things. I liked it, even though it made it a little bit harder to do my math homework.

I looked between the two of them, Mom and Dad, and thought about Eleanor, and that night I saw her eating dinner

Katie Mlinek

with her family. How flat the light was and everything. Our lights are the really warm, orange kind, mostly because they're cheaper, but they make everything look like a Christmas movie. I like our lights better, suddenly.

Comic Sans

Chapter 30

We were down to a couple of classes now to finish our presentations. Truthfully, about half the class was done theirs, which makes perfect sense. It really was a pretty easy project. I mean, we didn't need nearly all this time to get it done. The other half of the class – including our group – were the kids who messed around a bunch in the beginning, practically forgetting we really *did* have to make a presentation at some point.

Eleanor was taking care of all the design stuff, of course. Making stuff look all organized and nice. There's a certain orderliness to the way her brain works, I've noticed. The way her campaign posters are designed, the labels on her school folders, even her outfits: all crisp, color-coordinated, and understated. It just sort of came to me all of a sudden as I watched her layout the PowerPoint, even though I've known her all year and probably should have noticed a little sooner. It was a nice looking powerpoint is what I'm trying to get at.

Veronica was taking a nap on the floor underneath the table and Miranda kept swinging her feet and kicking Veronica's legs. Veronica literally growled under the table each time and shoved Miranda's legs away like an angry cow swatting at flies. Veronica must have been really tired. Miranda apologized each time but then always did it again two minutes later.

We had each done a section of the project and written down all our notes on paper to give to Eleanor, who was typing it all up. She was doing Mason's notes at the moment, and they were impossible to read. I know 'cause I was reading over her shoulder since there was nothing else to do. Chicken scratch isn't doing it justice. It looked more like cracks in a cement wall than actual writing.

"What does this word say?" Eleanor asked, tapping Mason on the shoulder. He looked up from his phone. This was maybe the fifth time she had asked that question.

"'Ophelia.' God, Eleanor, get a pair of reading glasses. You can even get them from a drugstore, but for the love of Christ, just get *something*." Mason went back to scrolling through his phone.

"I'm trying, okay? It's a little hard to read something from a person that never learned how to write."

Dang. Ellie was firing shots back. It's a little unnerving to see her so uncontrolled like this. Mason just snorted, but I think he knows she's the sheriff in town. Just then, Eleanor accidentally dropped all of the stacks of paper on the floor and it grazed Veronica ever so slightly. I mean, they hardly touched her, and they were just papers. But, of course, Veronica didn't care how little they had hit her. She immediately shoved all of the papers back at Eleanor's feet, bunching them all together.

"Thanks for the help," Eleanor sassed, picking the papers back up. I knew it would bother her, how crinkled they had just gotten. But man, she was being *vicious* today.

Suddenly, an announcement from the intercom system came on. This happens all the time. It's always to call someone to the office, or to let teachers know which room different meetings are in. It's pretty annoying, actually.

Comic Sans

"Could Eleanor Iding please report to Guidance. Repeat, Eleanor Iding to Guidance."

Everyone looked up for a moment. Eleanor and I looked at each other. That was a little rarer.

"What the heck could they need *me* for?" she said. "I'm pretty sure I haven't bullied anyone."

I could have pointed at two instances of bullying from the past thirty seconds, but figured it was best to hold my tongue.

"Make sure you take a buddy with you," Mrs. Desarrollee said with a smile from the front of the room.

"I'll walk you down to guidance and wait outside, okay?" I said. "It feels like someone died in here. I need fresh air."

"Sure." She nodded and we went down to the first floor, all the way to the guidance room. It was right in the corner of the school near the art room. I sat outside on the floor, tucked behind a trash can just so I'd be less noticeable. As I was sitting there, I started to notice how dirty the floor was. It was speckled with black dots, so all the dirt and junk isn't noticeable at all. But once you *really* look hard, you can see how much filth everyone sheds here. I can't imagine what an elementary school floor really looks like.

"What are you doing?!" someone barked. I peeked my head around the trash can and saw a teacher coming towards me. I quickly curled up against the trash can a little bit more, just in case he was talking to someone else and not me.

"Hey, you!" he said as he got closer. "Don't pretend you can't see me."

"I'm just waiting my turn," I said, pointing to the guidance room door. I looked through the glass panel wall and saw some

Katie Mlinek

pimpled freshman crying, holding a box of tissues. "I'm just going through a lot right now."

"Oh." The teacher's voice immediately softened. "Well, don't seem so sneaky, okay? You can probably wait inside, they have chairs."

"Okay," I said. "Thanks."

Man. If I always knew it was this easy to sucker people, I'd do it more often. And though I'd never met that teacher before, I already hope I don't have him next year. He seemed like a Grade A Jerk. *They have chairs.* Hey, thanks for the tip, buddy.

Finally, Eleanor came back out of guidance. She didn't notice me at first and stepped on my hand just a teeny little bit.

"Oh my gosh!" she said. "I'm so sorry! I didn't know you were right there!" She seemed a little put off. Or, as Mom would say, "all her razzle dazzle had been frazzled."

"It's okay, it's okay. So what happened in there?" I asked, standing up and brushing all the dirt off of my pants.

Eleanor clenched her teeth for a moment. "Someone vandalized one of my posters. They haven't even been up for a full week and someone already ruined one."

"What? What are you talking about?" I asked.

"The school officer told me. He said they're doing everything they can to 'handle the situation' and he thought I had the right to know."

"That's a load of crap."

"I know."

"Well, what did they write on the poster?"

Comic Sans

"You know the clown one? How it says 'This isn't a joke,' and then to vote for me? Well, they crossed the bottom part out and rewrote it so now it says, 'this isn't a joke, I smoke dope.'"

I laughed. "Sorry, I know it isn't funny, but –"

"I know, it's sort of funny because it's so stupid," she said. She practically spit out the word "stupid." This must be really, really bugging her. She unrolled the poster in her hand and showed it to me, and suddenly I was laughing uncontrollably.

"I can't believe it!" I said. The handwriting looked like a kindergartener's, and they drew a little joint coming out of Eleanor's mouth with smoke and all. I mean, I couldn't believe someone actually took the time to do that, to *Ellie* of all people. She's not the sort of person people ever talk about or even think about. I guess she's just always sort of *there*. And now to think that someone thought it worthwhile to mess up a poster to be class president…. I started laughing even harder. Eleanor just looked at me for a second, but then she, too, started cracking up. And soon we were both laughing so hard that it echoed down the hallways and she was almost crying.

"Thanks," she said. She started wiping away at the tears in the corner of her eyes. "I just – this is making me feel better. It *is* stupid. It really is."

"You know it."

"And now my stomach hurts from all that laughing."

"Good," I said. "Aren't you the one that told me laughing really hard increases your lifespan? Now you'll live longer to see more stupid things. Hold on one second." I ducked into the men's bathroom real quick and got a wad of paper towels. I came back out and handed them to her. "And you said you never cried."

She giggled again and dabbed the tears with a paper towel.

Katie Mlinek

"How much longer do you think I'll live?" she asked.

"Oh, so this is a soap opera now?" I said with a grin. "I think today just gave you two more years. Unless you really *are* smoking pot. Then you can take those years right back off."

Eleanor laughed and threw the paper towels away. "Finishing up this *project* is going to take those years back off," she said.

I shrugged. "I doubt it. C'mon, we'll go back there and I'll make sure everyone helps you get it done."

So we walked back to class, just the two of us. I swear, we would have been holding hands if either of us had the guts.

Comic Sans

Chapter 31

So Food Lion hasn't called me back, and I'm beginning to doubt I'll ever hear *anything* from the Dollar Tree (if it's even still around. The chances that it closed aren't that low). Even if I get the job from Smith's.... Okay. If I'm being honest with myself, I'd still take it. Begrudgingly, though! Begrudgingly. I'm still not quite over that whole mess. It's just too much to try to think about and fully resolve in my head, you know?

But then I started thinking, what if Smith's Gastro Pub *did* call, and Mom just didn't tell me? I mean, this wouldn't be the first time she didn't tell me something really important. What if all of the places called back and –

"James!" I snapped my head to see Mom at the kitchen doorway. My hand was halfway into a bag of chips. "Put those away. You're going to ruin your dinner."

I groaned and shoved the bag of chips back into the closet. I already knew we were having meatloaf for dinner, *which I hate*, by the way, though no one around here seems to care about that.

"What's for dinner tomorrow?" I asked. Maybe if it was something good like pizza, I'd have something to look forward to.

"I don't know," Mom called from the living room. "You and your dad are going to be on your own. My first day at Butterflake is tomorrow."

"What?" I came into the living room. My hand was still greasy from the chip bag. "Like the bakery? You're going to work there?"

"I just got the job today," Mom said, turning to look at me.

"Wow," I said. "Well, congratulations."

"Thanks," Mom said. She turned her back to me and I just stood at the door. I thought for a moment.

"Are you…excited?" I asked. It was weird how nonchalantly – and how little – Mom was talking about all of this. I mean, she loves baking and all, but I sort of thought her job search was over with Dad's prospects and everything.

"I'm glad, but I wouldn't say excited. I figure I'll work at Butterflake for a bit to make up for lost time," she said casually. *Lost time.* What, are we in crazy bad debt? I hope, at least, that if we're ever about to lose our house or something, Mom and Dad will tell me. So I don't just wake up one morning to see a bunch of random government guys going through everything we have and chucking it out onto the street, where they've put up a giant "Foreclosure" sign. At least that's how I imagine it would go.

"They told me they probably weren't hiring anytime soon when I went there, but hey, you never know how things are going to turn out," Mom said with a shrug.

"Does Dad know?" I asked.

"Of course he knows!" Mom shook her head and narrowed her eyes like I had just asked if we were moving to Mars. I mean, I feel like it's not a super ridiculous thing to ask, considering both of their track records. Asking if Dad knew, I mean. Though I wouldn't mind asking to move to Mars. As long as there was better A/C up there. Or really, any A/C at all.

I just nodded my head at Mom and decided I might as well actually go get on my bike and ride around for a bit. I needed something to distract me from eating, because I'm absolutely starving and Mom will kill me if she sees me trying to sneak food. And this development was...well, there's nothing a good bike ride can't help you get over.

I turned onto Edmunson Street, where I normally begin my little biking trips. Mom didn't seem too super thrilled about the whole job thing. Like I said, I know Mom loves baking and all, but...well, working at a bakery? I don't know much, but I do know that means a 3am alarm clock, long hours, and crappy customers who need their cake to be perfect for their precious daughter (who won't remember anything about her third birthday party). Is this the job she really wants? Is this why she went to college and got a degree in English? Is this what Mom wanted for her life?

And then I realized.

I don't have any plan. None at all. I probably became Mom's only plan, once her and Dad had me. I mean, she's been a stay-at-home mother all these years. But honestly, she probably had more of a plan than me at my age. There's nothing I'm super great at to form a plan around, though. I like to eat chips, and ride my bike, and I love the cooling feeling from wind hitting beads of sweat. You can't really make a career out of that. I'm no athlete. I'm not *anything*. Wow, that sounds cheesy. I've probably been watching too much of Mom's crappy TV shows with her.

So. This is what a crisis feels like. I've only ever heard of Eleanor having a crisis, and they're always "existential ones." I've never quite believed her because she has her life together more than anyone else I know. Ellie is going to be president of the student council (because if Alicia Stai wins, I will burn the school to the ground, starting with the yoga mats) and she is great as illustrating and designing and she's confident about it. Ellie knows who she is and what she likes and what to do with her life. What do I know? *Nothing*.

Katie Mlinek

I don't really have any "direction." It's another word Eleanor uses mostly, whenever she talks about going to the leadership convention or something. How it's in the "right direction." What is my right direction? Am I supposed to know now? I mean, if we're talking about right now, my only direction is to finish out junior year. But what then? Gah, I haven't even *thought* about college. I had that short period of time where I really cared about getting a job but nothing seems to have panned out and so what? I've given up. *I gave up.* Why did I stop at these three jobs I applied for? It's not like I looked *that* hard. And you know, I don't think there's much of a question about that being the wrong direction. That I decided not to care. Life is like a choose-your-own-adventure book, except it's choose-your-own-emotions and no matter what we all end up dead anyways. The problem is, I can't choose anything. I feel, I don't know, stuck? Like my suit under my bike tires.

I mean, think about it. Everything I've done this year has sort of been a waste. Really, I haven't done anything at all this year. Nothing worthwhile, at least. I've focused on stupid things – like getting a suit, having my phone back – and then it disintegrates right through my fingers. Like freaking snow in my hands. I just give up. Isn't this the time of my life that I'm supposed to start figuring things out? I haven't even *tried*. If I keep telling myself I'll deal with things later, what if that "later" comes and I still haven't done anything? And Eleanor couldn't even name a font for me. There are thousands of fonts out there (and I know because she's showed me hundreds), and she couldn't name one for me.

Man, life was so easy back before Dad lost his job, and we had a nice, cozy routine, and Mom would do her volunteering and Dad would do his driving thing and I would do my school thing and that was that. You know who I really want to talk to more than anything right now? Eleanor. But I can't. I can bike anywhere in this whole neighborhood but I can't just go past her house, or even knock on the door. And I hate myself for it.

    I want to play with Lucas again at Mr. Greg's house and read *If You Give a Mouse a Cookie* to Mom and watch out the window for Dad to come home from a long trip away. I mean, I do really need a job and all, but if I'm being honest with myself – I don't want one. Not really. I don't want to have to think about college next year, or summer conferences in Denver, or having some job to wake up for every day. Why did Dad have to lose his job? Why did Mom have to lose her mind once stuff got even slightly hard? And why, *why* did I have to be stuck in the middle of it?

Katie Mlinek

Chapter 32

Ellie wasn't at school the next day. I first was concerned because I didn't see her on that spot on the staircase like I normally do. I get kind of nervous towards the end of second period because I know I'm about to see her for the only time that day. I always pack up my stuff way too early and then I kind of loiter in class for about a minute, and that way we normally pass each other on the same spot on the staircase every time. There are some days where we pass each other higher on the staircase because she left class late, others where she's super early and we pass each other just as I'm leaving my classroom. But today I didn't pass her at all. So I figured she just wasn't at school. I was really eager to get to English class so I could see if she was there or not, but then I didn't even get a chance to go. I was called down for a stupid Student Assessment.

I hate those. It's where you're called down to guidance and you have to answer a ton of questions about administration, how helpful guidance is, your teachers' teaching strategies, your schedule, how clean the cafeteria tables are – really, really stupid stuff like that. I'm always called down at least once per year, though they say they choose students at random. I swear, all those people in the guidance office have nothing to do all day long except launch full investigations against poster vandalism and these horrible surveys. It's really just an excuse for our school to tell every other school that we're great, because students are too squeamish to low-score anything. But anyways, I was really bummed I missed English.

Comic Sans

As if that wasn't enough of my problems, Eleanor didn't show up the day after that, either. It wasn't as horrible, sitting there with just Mason and Miranda and Veronica as I thought it would be, and they somehow had Ellie's password to get onto the PowerPoint and keep editing it. They really didn't need me. So I ended up telling Mrs. Desarollee that I felt sick and needed to go to the nurse, and then I just wandered around the halls with my pass. I'm glad she forgot to tell me to take a buddy with me. The funny thing is, I sort of *did* start to feel really sick while walking around. I even stopped in the bathroom for a second in case I had to puke, but I didn't. So I just kept walking around and let my heart skip a beat whenever I saw one of Eleanor's posters up on a corkboard. There was a blank spot where they had to take the vandalized one down. Thinking about it again made me laugh to myself so much that I almost felt better.

I don't know any of Ellie's friends, and it's not like I have any way of calling her since her phone number is in my "lost" cellphone, so I have no way of finding out if she's okay or not. She's probably just sick. She would have told me if she was going on some crazy trip or something. She actually does tell me a lot. Just talk, you know. But I like it. I like that she feels comfortable enough to tell me weird little mundane things about her life. Like if her cereal was too soggy in the morning or something. One time she told me this huge, fifteen minute story about how she lost her favorite pencil and spent an entire afternoon looking for it. It's the sort of story that's supposed to be really boring. But the way she told it, I don't know, it just *wasn't*.

After a while I started to think that maybe Mrs. Desarollee might get suspicious. She's the sort of person who times how long it takes for a student to use the bathroom to make sure they didn't run off to smoke weed or something. I mean she's nice and everything, but it doesn't make sense for her to give us months for a project to just mess around and then get mad if we're in the

Katie Mlinek

bathroom for too long. So I turned around and headed back to the English classroom, clutching the hall pass in my hand.

When I walked back into class and over to my group (Mrs. Desarollee didn't say anything – phew), I realized that Mason was gone. Miranda and Veronica were working together quietly, Miranda reading her notes to Veronica and Veronica hunt-and-peck typing them onto the PowerPoint. They turned around as I came.

"Oh, James! How are you? Are you feeling better?" Miranda asked.

"Yeah," I said, "loads better. What are you guys doing?"

"Finishing up this stupid presentation. Mason is over in the corner," Veronica said, nodding her head in his direction. I looked over to see him sitting at his desk, working on math homework.

"Why is he in the corner?" I asked.

"Because he's in timeout," Miranda said.

"What?" I remembered the temper tantrum I apparently missed the other week, and how red his face gets in gym class.

"Miranda's just joking," Veronica said. "We're almost done. We're just trying to finish up the work Eleanor had been doing. There's nothing really else to do."

"You're being consistent about the fonts and stuff, right?" I asked. "Because if she comes back and you guys have changed it a lot, she might just lose her mind."

"Oh, Miranda changed everything," Veronica said, jabbing a thumb in the direction of a giggling Miranda. "But I have a little friend called Control Z. So we're all good."

I laughed. "So is there anything I can do?"

"Nope. Just go hang with Mason and we'll finish it up."

Comic Sans

I nodded and went over to my right near Mason. I pulled out some study guide I got for the gym test – I know, a test in *gym*, it's crazy – and looked over at Mason. He saw me holding the study guide and held his up, which he must have been working on, and guffawed. I smiled at him.

"Listen up, everyone!" Mrs. Desarollee said. Everyone stopped talking in their groups and looked over at the teacher. "I almost forgot, you all have to vote for your class officers today. I've got the ballots up at the front of the room. Take one, fill it out, and put it in this yellow bin right here. And please, don't put your name on it. So many students put their name on it every year. It's supposed to be anonymous. Okay, that's all, you can get back to work now."

I immediately went up and grabbed a ballot from the front. It was sort of weird to see Eleanor's name on a paper surrounded by a bunch of people I didn't know, or barely knew. But the weirdest thing was seeing Alicia Stai's name right next to Eleanor's. I looked over at Alicia and saw her riding piggy-back on some guy whose name I think is Brad. She was squealing as if she really was a pig, and I swear, her stupid fake eyelashes were in danger of falling out. I groaned, put down my increasingly-important vote for Ellie, put a little tick mark next to the names that sounded the nicest for the other positions, and laid it gently in the yellow bin. The only other paper in there was Mason's, and I know because he put his name on it. But I noticed, before setting my own ballot on top, that he had chosen Ellie for president. I just left my ballot on top, went back to my seat, and kept working on the study guide. I thought for a moment about checking the other ballots as students put them in, and if I could find a way to change them in case they voted for someone other than Eleanor. But really, there's no way even I could pull off something that crazy.

Katie Mlinek

Chapter 33

Mom had the radio playing in the kitchen again, wearing those pearl earrings she loved so much, which I only realized because she kept reaching up to touch them and twirl them or whatever. Dad was reading a book in the living room, and occasionally Mom would come in with a mixing bowl or spatula or something and say a bunch of stuff, then go back to whatever she was baking.

I had just come in from biking. I hadn't biked around the neighborhood in a while, and it was nice to get out again when the sky is turning to that heavy blue and you can actually feel the temperature dropping. It's my favorite time of the day. Sunsets are just a little overrated. I think the moment right *after* a sunset is the best part. It's a shade of blue that you just can't find anywhere else. It's like looking into the ocean, when you're way out in the middle and you can't see land anymore and you look down and all you see is blue, but you can still feel how deep it is, how much life is in it. When you look up into a sky like that, you can really believe there are billions of stars out there. Once I almost hit Beard-Os mailbox, back before it disappeared, because I forgot to look back down. I still feel embarrassed just thinking about it.

I had biked far away from Eleanor's house, though all I wanted was to run straight to it. I wish I could. I wish it was socially acceptable. But the last time I went there, I wasn't exactly at my most impressive, and for me to come running up to her

Comic Sans

doorsteps soaked in sweat, all paranoid that her life is in danger…well, they might as well tie me up and quarter me with a bunch of horses. Eleanor's the one that taught me all about that. Cool ways governments used to torture people. She told me once about how back in Ancient Greece, they would put people inside a giant bull made of brass and cook them *alive*. That's how I feel on most hot days, going between our house with no A/C to our school with no A/C *and* small, pathetic triangle windows. But nights like tonight, where it's all cool and springish, the only torture I feel is not knowing if Ellie's okay or not.

When I came back in, Mom had flour all over her forehead. She must have gotten some on her hand then tried to push her hair back. But she didn't seem to notice.

"Good, you're back, come help me start cleaning up some dishes."

I came into the kitchen and saw piles of bowls and pans and pots stacked so dangerously in the sink, I swear they were about to fall over and crash through the floor.

"Gee, Mom, are you baking for the whole neighborhood or something?" I asked.

"No. We're having pizza! I'm making enough to last us the next couple of days, too," Mom said proudly. "Butterflake inspired me."

I remembered her plan to make pizza now. The other day I had to go to the grocery store with her and instead of getting everything she needed from each aisle and proceeding from one to the next, she was running around the place like a madman, forgetting flour or eggs or tomatoes or sausages and I was practically jogging by the end of it. She wouldn't even split up her shopping list with me to cut the time in half.

Katie Mlinek

"So…since Dad is going to get a job now and everything and you've got the bakery gig…can we start using the dishwasher?" I asked.

The phone rang and Mom jumped.

"Can you get that, hon?" she hollered.

I heard Dad's faint reply and Mom turned back to me.

"Nice try," she said. "You know, with just the three of us here, we ended up not really needing the dishwasher after all. I don't know why we had it in the first place. You can wash dishes every once in a while, can't you, James?" Mom grinned.

"I don't know if I can live that oppressed," I said, laughing.

"Wow. Some son I've raised," Mom said. Dad came into the kitchen and Mom flicked some of the water on her hands at him. "I blame you, too!" She laughed and I laughed but Dad was not laughing. Something was up. Immediately, Mom wiped her hands off and sat him down.

"What's wrong?" she asked. She motioned for me to turn the radio off and I did.

"I didn't get the job."

I froze. The water was still running and soap slid down the pan. Mom just looked at Dad, but Dad wasn't looking at her. His head was hanging low, and he didn't say anything else.

"That was them on the phone?"

He nodded.

Mom had a wash rag still in her hands that she squeezed and let go again and again. A little bit of water trickled to the floor.

"Honey…I'm so sorry."

Comic Sans

I felt everything inside of me drop like an anvil. I turned the water off but my hands were still all soapy.

"This was supposed to be the end. This was going to be the part where things start getting better," Dad said.

"It doesn't work like that. I wish like hell it did. But it doesn't." Mom looked at Dad with her wide, brown eyes. It was weird, hearing Mom even say something as close to cursing as "hell." There was something new in Mom's face, a kind of earnestness that stuck itself to every word she said. Dad didn't say anything.

"Well, listen. This isn't a dead end. This isn't *any* kind of end," Mom said. Dad still wasn't making eye contact with her. I couldn't tell if they remembered I was in the room or not, but it was too awkward, too serious a time to leave.

"They hired some other guy today. Instead of me," Dad said.

"And somewhere, down the line, someone will hire you instead of another guy. It's going to happen, David. And you're not going through this alone. Right, James?" Mom turned and looked at me and pulled a chair out. I came over and sat down with them. I cleared my throat – it had closed up more than I realized.

"Yeah," I croaked. I cleared my throat again. "You've got us."

"He's exactly right." Mom paused for a moment. We waited to see how Dad would react to any of this, but he wasn't at all. Whatever was going on in his head he was burying deep down. Mom looked at the floor, thinking. She lifted her head to speak again. "Now listen. I love you both very, very much," she said. "You two are all that matter to me in this entire world. You both make me *so* proud. And dangit, if we can't get through this together, we're not a real family. But I'm not concerned about that. Because I *know* we'll be okay. I know it's not ever going to be easy. Nothing should be. But what matters is that I love you, and

Katie Mlinek

you both love me, and some other guy isn't going to put us into ruins. He can't. Every missed job, every sacrifice, all these scrutinous looks at money every month – they're for each other. Like I said. We're family."

She was practically monologuing but I didn't care. I felt like something important was happening. Mom was right. We *are* family, as small and disconnected as we sometimes might be. And I do know they'll always be there for me, even if maybe I don't fully know what I'm doing with my life.

"I love you," Dad said, looking up at her. He looked over at me. "I just want to support you two. I know I'm letting you both down."

"You're not. The only way in which you could let James and I down is if you give up on yourself, or get wrapped up in worrying that you've failed us somehow. That's the only way. Didn't get this job? That's fine. Don't get the next one? That's fine, too. It will work out in the end. And we'll still have each other. And that's all that matters. That's it. That's all there is."

"Mom's right," I said. I didn't have to clear my throat this time.

Dad nodded. "I know. I know. I...I'll do anything for you two. I will."

"We know." Mom smiled and squeezed Dad's shoulder. He smiled back and then the oven went off.

"That's the pizza! Set out plates and napkins, my dears. I think this is going to be a good batch of pizzas right here."

Dad and I got up and helped clear away the kitchen some more. Mom turned the radio back on and I washed the soap off of my hands. It was completely dark outside now, but through the window, if you looked really, really hard, you could just start to see some stars.

Comic Sans

Chapter 34

The rest of the week went by and still no Ellie. I was already reciting in my head what I would say if I found out she had cancer. I mean, a week is a long time to just sort of disappear from school. And I didn't hear anyone talking about it, so it stayed a mystery.

By Monday, I was just really nervous. I hardly ever get really nervous about stuff, like sick-to-your-stomach nervous, and I can't tell you why I am now. Okay, I can. I was definitely nervous about Ellie. Because if she wasn't there, that would mean something was really seriously wrong and I just don't know what I'd do about it. Probably start searching through every local hospital's records to see if I could find her name somewhere. But seriously, what would I bring her if I found out she was horribly sick with some crippling disease? Of course, my mind immediately jumped to doing something with fonts, but I just can't. I would get it all wrong and she'd smile politely and appreciate the thought but deep down it would hurt her sensibilities. And why am I even thinking about something as horrible as Eleanor being in the hospital? I'm ridiculous.

When I didn't see her on the stairs again, my entire day became a dreadful build-up to English class, which was the only way I'd find out if Eleanor was really here or not. I felt like I was losing my mind – I'd see the back of a brunette's head, or a nose that slightly curved upwards out of the corner of my eye, and immediately think it was her. Maybe it's worth checking my temperature again.

When I walked into English class, Eleanor wasn't there. I felt my heart sink deep into the pit of my stomach. I guess I sort of knew that this would happen, and yet I had let myself hope anyways. I sat down with my group in the corner.

And that's when I remembered that we had to give our presentations to the class today. There's one kid in the class whose name I honestly never remember who was wearing a tie. A *tie*. Even Mrs. Desarrollee should be able to see through crap like that.

Now that I was paying a little more attention, I noticed how restless the entire class was. It was the pre-presentation jitters. I haven't paid any attention to many people since this project began, and now I'm suddenly aware of everyone again. In the middle of the room, Alicia Stai was sitting cross-legged on top of the desk, picking enamel off the top of it with her fingernails, chatting with some members of the Slut Club. And to think she dared try to be president of the student council? It's sickening, really. Why would she want to be in something like student council? And all that enamel-picking counts as destruction to school property, right?

Just then, Eleanor walked through the door. She came in with such a flurry I almost felt a breeze from outside come in with her. She came over and sat down next to me, and her nose was a little bit pink at the tip, like a rabbit. Like the first time I really noticed her, back when this terribly long project began.

"Hi," she said, sitting down. Her voice was gruff, as if she had been smoking a pack of cigarettes every day for the past ten years.

"Ellie!" I said. "Are you okay, where were you?"

"I was sick."

Comic Sans

"Well, now you have an English presentation," Mason said.

"Shut up," I said, laughing a little. I turned back to Ellie. "That is pretty serious, though. Are you sure you should be in school?"

"Yeah, it wasn't bad, as far as pneumonia goes. And I knew we had the presentation today. And they announce the new class president after school, too. So I figured I should be here," Eleanor said. She coughed a little bit and tried to cover it up.

"Listen, you don't have to present anything, just rest here, okay?" I said. "We've got this covered."

"We didn't give you anything to read, just in case you wouldn't show up," Miranda said. She gave Eleanor a big hug, squeezing her so much that she started to cough.

"Okay, okay, that's enough, let her breathe," I said. Miranda let her go, gave her one last quick side hug, and then sat back down.

"You probably have pneumonia now," Veronica said. Miranda just shrugged.

The first group did their presentation on Macbeth, and they botched it. I kept looking over at Eleanor, hoping that we would make eye contact and laugh together whenever one of the presenters said something stupid. But she just sat there with her chin in her hand and a faraway smile on her face. I wondered what she was thinking about. Like that maybe she was happy to see me again or something. But I'm being stupid, she couldn't have been thinking that – she was probably just wishing she was home again, like everyone else.

Then it was our group's turn to present. Mason strutted to the front of the room almost the instant the last group finished, and I think Miranda got distracted by dust on the floor or something before we got up there. Veronica looked like a cat that had been dragged into a bubble bath. Eleanor tried to put in a last word urging us to let her go up and present, too (and really, I don't blame her. We were a rough crew walking up there). I made her stay, though. She coughed a little in defiance, but didn't get up from her seat.

Miranda had little notecards with her that she was reading off of, but to me it just looked like a bunch of abstract lines row after row. When she finished her slide, Mason moved onto the next one and then it was my turn. I caught eyes with Eleanor for a moment, who gave me a brief thumbs up. If the class wondered why I started smiling like a fool in the midst of talking about Hamlet's suicidal thoughts, they didn't say anything.

And so the presentation went on just like that, Mason, Miranda, Veronica and I all taking turns talking about each slide, and in under fifteen minutes we were done. A few kids woke up while the rest gave polite little golf claps, and we went back to our seats as if we were the same as ever. But I felt a little different, for some reason. Like an era of my life was over. What were Ellie and I going to do now that the project was over? What was our whole group going to do? This project was the only thing keeping all of us together.

The rest of class dragged by as each group did their presentation. Mrs. Desarollee promised us that the second half of groups would have time to present during the next class, and everyone groaned just as they had when she announced the project two months ago.

As most days, we had the last five minutes of class to pack-up, which really meant that we had the last five minutes of class to just hang out and do whatever we wanted.

"You guys did great," Eleanor said, turning to all of us. "And thanks for finishing up the presentation. I'm glad I had sent a picture of those notes to the group chat all that time ago as a back-up. It ended up coming in handy."

Comic Sans

I hadn't even thought about that the last couple of classes. How Eleanor had *all* of our notes with her and everything. I kept forgetting – or repressing – the fact that they all still talked to each other over the group chat all the time. She must have sent them everything. I wasn't a part of any of that.

"It was no problem," Veronica said with a shrug.

"It was interesting watching each of your different presenting styles," Ellie said. "Like how Miranda, you were so chipper that I sort of wanted to give you The Daily Squeeze. Truly." Everyone laughed and Miranda blushed.

"Well, I think *I* really come alive when I give presentations," Veronica said cheekily.

"My inner businessman comes out. I just imagine I'm taking control over a conference and it all comes together," Mason said.

"Well, James? What are you? C'mon, you can't sit this one out," Miranda said.

"I just…read. Like a normal person," I said bluntly. Now that I think about it, I was pretty boring. Or *am* pretty boring, I should say. Everyone still laughed, though.

"You're about as opposite from normal as it gets," Eleanor said.

"Oh yeah? Look at me. I'm wearing a T-shirt and jeans. I have no hobbies. My *name* is even normal. And I present normal, too," I said, giving her a nudge. Just playing around and all. It didn't bug me. Really, it didn't. Really.

"Aww, James, I think you're special," Miranda said.

"Well, gee, thanks, I *feel* special now," I said, giving her a good eye roll. I laughed. This whole thing was starting to get awkward quick. I just sound whiny, like I'm fishing for compliments or something. I'm no fishmonger.

Katie Mlinek

Eleanor was looking at me with narrowed eyes and I could tell she was thinking really intensely about something. She coughed a bit and shook her head.

"What?" I asked.

She looked at me. "What what?"

"What as in what was that look you were giving me?"

Eleanor shrugged and gave a sly smile. "I wasn't giving you any *look*," she said with another cough.

"You definitely were. It was one of those 'I can see your soul right now' looks. Well, don't keep looking, I don't have one."

Eleanor laughed. "What if I said I *could* see your soul?"

"Well, what do you see?"

"Comic Sans."

Mason started cracking up. "She just called you stoo-pid," he guffawed.

"Not at all. I just gave him the highest compliment I could," Eleanor said. "You're still the Impact font, Mason."

"I don't know what any of that means, but I feel insulted," Mason said.

"You should be," Veronica said. And, mimicking him, "she just called you stoo-pid."

Eleanor laughed, which quickly turned into another cough. I just looked at her.

"Comic Sans?" I asked.

She nodded. "It means you're not like anybody else, and that's enough."

Comic Sans

I thought about that for a second, but it didn't make a ton of sense, especially since when I think of Comic Sans, I think of kindergarten classroom papers and first grade birthday party invitations.

Though, you know, sometimes we still get papers in high school with Comic Sans. And it really sticks out because it's just so different from the normal, plain, default fonts. It feels like laughing after a good cry. Which isn't a feeling I'm super familiar with, since I don't cry much. Probably even less than Eleanor says she does. Girls always exaggerate about how much or how little they cry.

If there was one thing I was positive about, it's that having Eleanor back – even though she's still clearly sick – is nice.

"You sound like you're still sick," I said, trying to joke again. "Sure you took enough medicine?"

She smiled, which is always a relief when I make terrible, terrible jokes. I didn't deserve it. I really didn't.

"Guys." Miranda looked up at all of us as if she's just had a sudden realization. "What are we going to do? Now that it's the end of the year and all? What if we don't have any classes with each other after this?"

"Most friendships like this don't last," Veronica said. "It's like gym class buddies. You're friends out of necessity."

"I don't know…I feel like…well, I like you all a lot," Eleanor said with her raspy voice. "Just because the project is over doesn't mean our little group is over."

"You guys can come see plays at The Scruta," Mason said. We all just looked at him. "Really. I can get you all in for free every once in a while. And we can go get ice cream afterwards or something. We can do that during summer sometime."

Katie Mlinek

"That sounds awesome!" Miranda said. "Do they have moose tracks, though? That's my favorite kind of ice cream."

Eleanor looked down. "I'm going to Denver for the summer," she said.

"What?" Everyone looked over at her.

"You guys didn't know that?" I asked.

"You told James but not us?" Miranda asked. I could tell they were a little upset and all, but it sort of made me feel good. That she told me and trusted me and wanted me to know and all that. I just shrugged.

"It's just one summer," Eleanor said. "My parents really want me to go and everything."

"What are you doing there?" Veronica asked.

"A leadership conference. It's stupid, really, I know. But I'll make the best of it." She stopped and looked at all of us. "And I'll still talk to you guys every day."

"Promise?" Miranda asked.

"Pinky promise." Eleanor held out her pinky and they pinky swore.

"You guys have to each kiss each other's pinkies or else it doesn't count," Veronica said.

"Very funny," Eleanor said, "but then Miranda would get sick and her summer would be ruined, too."

"This is going to be a good summer no matter what," Miranda said.

That really struck me, for some reason. That Miranda could go from being all upset about Eleanor to being positive her summer would still be good just the same. It seemed sort of wise,

Comic Sans

for some reason, but maybe Miranda is just really mentally off and I'm stupid enough to construe it as wisdom. I would do that. I really would.

Chapter 35

I went on to my physics class afterwards, convinced the hallways were at least brighter now that Eleanor was back. I walked in just as the late bell rang, took my usual seat in the back, and suffered through forty-five minutes of absolute boredom.

Physics is the worst class. Well, not the worst. Just the most boring. It's really easy and dumbed down and everything, and we just take notes straight from the PowerPoint each day. It's about as easy as learning sight words in kindergarten. I just sit in the back and do nothing and sometimes take a nap, which at least helps the time go by slightly faster.

Since the class is so quick and easy, we almost always finish a couple of minutes before the bell rings. But the end-of-the-day announcements came even earlier than that.

"Attention everyone," the voice said, which I soon recognized as Mr. Zander's, "we have the results of the student council elections in and are now going to share them with everyone. Teachers, please make sure your students quiet down for this important announcement."

Everyone settled into their seats and our teacher barked at the students already standing by the door ready to leave. I perked up. Eleanor must be stressing out like crazy right now.

"Alright," my principal said, coming back on the intercom, "I'll begin with the underclassmen positions."

He went through the whole list of arbitrary positions only open to underclassmen, naming even the runner-ups, as if that would make the losers feel any better. I waited with bated breath for Eleanor's name to be called as he moved on to the list of actually meaningful student council positions. If I thought those presentations felt like forever, this list was even longer. Once the class realized there was nothing to listen for, they all started to talk, loud enough that I had to strain my ears to listen. Secretaries, treasurers, historians, and social media coordinators later, he finally got to the presidential announcement.

"And the student council president is…" he paused. I waited. "Eleanor Iding! And the runner-up was Alicia Stai. Great effort, Alicia. Students, please continue waiting for the bell to ring for class dismissal.

I bolted out of my seat. I don't even know why. I was just so excited for Eleanor, that she was in school and that she was the president just like she wanted and everything. I left the room without my teacher even noticing amongst the chaos of our class and, barely even thinking, found myself walking towards Ellie's math class. I didn't have anything planned. I don't know what I expected. I just sort of *went* there.

As luck had it, just as I was nearing her classroom door, Eleanor popped out. She started to turn the other direction at first, but then noticed me and stopped. She had a big grin on her face.

"Ellie! Congratulations!" I said, throwing my arms wide. She came over and gave me a hug.

"Thanks," she said, her voice still. She looked up at me and smiled. I was thankful she didn't ask what I was doing there.

"We need to celebrate right now. Pronto. ASAP," I said.

"There's not much you can do in a hallway," she said. "I just have to run to the bathroom and then talk to my teacher after class. I missed a lot last week. I think we're in a whole different unit but I'm not even sure." She coughed.

"Why don't you come over for dinner tonight?" I asked. It just kind of popped out of me, like a sneeze you aren't expecting. "You know. To celebrate."

Eleanor paused for a moment. "I mean, I have a lot of work to —"

"Don't worry about that," I said. "You already *did* a lot of work. And now you need to kick back and celebrate it."

"My parents...I don't...." Eleanor looked at me hesitantly and suddenly I felt like the biggest doofus on this whole planet. To think I could break the weird boundary between our two houses. It's ridiculous. *I'm* ridiculous. I had no chance.

"Well, you know, school is almost over for the year and then I won't see you for a couple of months. And you live pretty close, right?" She smiled. "My parents should be fine."

I gave her my house address and told her to come at seven. She could just leave her bike next to mine and ring on the doorbell and I'd be there. She thanked me and started to go back into her math class. "You know," she said, stopping to look at me. I just looked back.

"What?" I asked.

She just shook her head. "You're just amazing. That's all." And she went into math.

I guess she forgot about using the bathroom.

Walking back, the halls felt like the closest I would ever get to walking in heaven. When I walked back into my physics class, though, it was chaos. There were still just a couple of minutes till

Comic Sans

the bell rang and kids were standing near the door again, ready to go. I went to my seat in the back of the room and sunk into it, happy about everything.

Katie Mlinek

Chapter 36

Now the one thing that for some reason I hadn't considered was how my parents were going to respond to this whole having-a-girl-over-for-dinner-last-minute thing. On my way home from school, I tried to play the scene over and over again in my head, so that I would be prepared for any scenario. Dad sends me to my room? I'll train a pigeon to send a letter to Eleanor's house. Mom starts lecturing me? I'll pretend to have a stroke in the middle of it. So yeah. Anything and everything might go wrong.

I walked into my house hesitantly, creaking the door open and peeking my head around it. I came inside and took my shoes off.

"James? Is that you?" my mom called.

"Yeah," I said.

"How was school?" Mom walked out of the living room and immediately picked up the shoes that I had just taken off.

"It was fine," I said, "where's Dad?"

"In the living room watching TV."

I walked into the living room and sat down on a couch opposite Dad. I watched the show with him for a moment. It was some guy with a big, wiry mustache talking about cars. The cars were dirty, the guy's beard was dirty, even the lens on the camera they were filming with was dirty. It was just an all-around gross show that only a trucker would like. But it was the sort of thing that made my dad feel better, I was sure of it. It wouldn't depress the heck out of him.

I picked up a book from the coffee table. Hopefully I could start pretending to read the book and sneak glances at him to figure out what sort of mood he was in. But Dad didn't seem to be in any mood at all. He just sat there, watching the TV with no particular expression on his face or anything. He was giving me nothing. I accidentally dropped the book on the floor and reached down for it.

"Oh, hey, James, didn't notice you come in," Dad said, pausing the TV. "How was school?"

"Good, good. It was fine."

"Good. Hey. Go up to your room."

I looked over at Dad, startled. I hadn't even *said* anything yet!

Dad started cracking up. "Don't look so scared. I have a surprise for you up there."

Curious, I left my book bag in the living room and went up to my room. I was a little nervous still. I was running through my head all of the possibilities of what could be in my room. Maybe that chocolate cereal that Mom won't let me get?

I walked into my room. There, plugged in proudly and rotating back and forth, was a new fan. Dad came up the stairs behind me.

"Well?"

I turned to him. "This is awesome!" I couldn't believe it. I can actually sleep and not sweat all of my body fat away now.

Katie Mlinek

Dad grinned. "I realized I wanted you to survive this summer, and no A/C is pretty tough. Tim Cunningham down the road had this old rinky dink broken thing and I offered to take it off his hands and fix it up. And now it works like a charm. It even rotates! See how it glides?"

I laughed. "Yeah, Dad, it's pretty cool. How did you know how to fix a fan?"

He shrugged. "I know a thing or two."

Dad was beaming, and I was so happy – not just that I had a fan, but that he went through the trouble and thought to get me one.

Now at least I don't have to worry about sweating bullets before Eleanor comes over. That was another thing I hadn't thought about. How gross I'd be sitting in this sauna of a house before she came over.

Of course, now I was nervous again about asking Dad. Dad's not the sort of guy who will say yes to anything just because he's in a good mood. Mom does that, though. Mom wakes up in good moods – which is really alien to me, I don't know how she does it – and when I was younger, I used to ask her if I could have a piece of Halloween candy in the morning. She said yes *all the time*. It was great.

But having Eleanor over for dinner is a completely different matter. And I could feel my face starting to get red already.

"Well, I won't just stand here, I'll let you enjoy your new fan," Dad said.

"Thanks," I said, "for the fan and everything."

"No problem," Dad said with a smile. He turned and started walking down the stairs.

"Hey, Dad," I said, walking after him to the top of the stairs.

Comic Sans

"Yeah?"

"You remember my English class group? For *Hamlet*?"

"Yeah."

"And you remember that girl Eleanor?" Dad paused. "Mom met her once," I said quickly.

"I don't remember anything about an Eleanor."

"Well, she's in my English class group and she's really nice and hardworking and she lives in this neighborhood now and we're really good friends and all."

"Okay?" Dad said.

"Is it alright if she comes over for dinner tonight?"

Dad just looked at me for a second and I panicked. "I mean, she just won this big thing to be the president at our school and stuff and she worked really hard on it and everything and her parents kind of suck so I was sort of hoping that we could celebrate here, you know, just with a nice dinner or something. I'll make it! I'll make dinner. You guys don't have to do anything. We can eat it outside! On the driveway! We could do that!"

Mom walked in at the bottom of the stairs right in the middle of it. "What is this? You told your father about a girl and not me?"

"He hardly told me anything, but if she comes over tonight, we'll have no choice but to know all about her," Dad said with a laugh.

I looked at Mom helplessly. "Sorry, Mom, I don't know, I just –" I was at a loss for words now. But Mom laughed and shared a look with Dad.

"What's her favorite food?" Dad asked.

Katie Mlinek

"What?"

"I mean, what would she like to eat? For dinner?"

"Oh." Funny enough, I hadn't even thought about that. I racked my brain for any memory of her mentioning food, like dinner food, but all I could remember was her gushing at the neighborhood block party about eating macaroni and cheese on the night before Thanksgiving, but not the Kraft kind, it was something different, some brand....

"Velveeta," I said. "She likes the cheesy Velveeta stuff."

"Any girl that likes cheap food is fine by me," Dad said.

"That's the kind that's basically just American cheese melted over noodles, right? I'll go get some at the store right now," Mom said. Why were my parents being so cool about this?

"No, Mom, don't worry about it, I can find something else for us to eat no problem," I said.

"I was going to go to the store anyways. And you know!" She snapped her fingers, which I hardly ever see Mom do. "I have brownies from the bakery that we didn't sell yesterday! They might be a bit stale but you two can have it as dessert."

"That's great, we can just have the brownies for dinner! We don't need to get anything," I said.

"Absolutely not, you can't invite a girl over and then not feed her," Mom said.

"What time is she coming?" Dad asked.

"Is seven okay?"

"That's plenty of time," Mom said. "Let me just grab my purse real quick...and oh! Did you ever call Food Lion back?"

"Food Lion called?"

"Yeah. And you need to call back about coming in for your first day of training," Mom said.

"What? You didn't tell me that!" Any irritation I felt from Mom not remembering something as important as Food Lion calling dissipated immediately. I had a job. I was going to have something to do this summer, something real and worthwhile and "in the right direction." *I had a job.*

"I left the number on the counter," Mom said.

"I'll call them right now, I promise," I said.

I called Food Lion up just as my mom was running out the door and promised to show up the coming Saturday for my first round of training. As I hung up the phone, Dad patted me on the back while walking by. I had nothing to worry about this whole time. It felt like spring suddenly, even though it was pretty solidly hot and summer.

I can't believe my parents were being so calm and supportive about this. And I guess that makes me pretty lucky. Both of them just setting everything aside for me all of a sudden. I guess they have always done that all this time. And you know, no matter what happens, I have them. At the end of the day, that's all there is.

When Mom got back, she taught me how to get the water to boil fast, which I had never even done before, and she set the table with place napkins and everything. And when Eleanor came and knocked on the door, she was wearing the same outfit from school but had put a little clip in her hair and was beautiful. And she came into my house and met my parents and we all sat down to a Velveeta dinner together. I wasn't worried about having to keep the A/C off for the whole summer, or not getting my phone back, or how long it would take for Dad to get a job. I wasn't worried about Eleanor living near me or not living near me. I wasn't worried about being a Comic Sans kind of person. I wasn't

Katie Mlinek

worried about Mom or Dad because I knew together we were all happy. And American cheese had never tasted so good.

Comic Sans

ACKNOWLEDGEMENTS

First of all, special thanks to all of the friends and family that have offered support, encouragement, interest, or just let me rant for hours on end. You may not even realize just how much a kind thought here or there meant, but sometimes it was my only reason to plop myself into that writing chair. Thanks to: Aunt Becky and Uncle Dante, Grandma and Grandpa, Uncle Michael and Aunt Colleen, Aunt Rachel and Uncle Josh, Natalie Hale, Viviana Prado-Núñez, Khalid Ali, the Regal Westminster 9 crew, Teddie Venetoulis, and Grace Meredith. Thanks to Rachel and the loving employees at La Cakerie for the endless coffee, cozy couch, and good conversation to help with my book. Thanks to everyone who let me pick their brains at one point or another: Sam Owens, Nick Handel, Vinny Sacchetti, Chris Harding, and Joseph McFadden.

Huge thanks to my incredibly talented cover artist, Flynn Walkinshaw. Any books that sell at all are because of you.

Thanks to Elana Rubin, who was the first ever person to lay eyes on this novel and, amazingly, didn't run for the hills.

Ruthe – half of this book was written sitting next to you and a cup of Zeke's coffee. I wouldn't have wanted to sit anywhere else.

Becky – you are the rock that lets this world keep on rolling. You and your Schmuman-ness keeps me going.

Daniel Roy – I don't even know how to thank you enough for all of the selfless time you put into reading my drafts again and again and again, then changing my website again and again and again. There aren't enough cat memes in this world to repay you.

Thanks to my dad, Christopher Mlinek. I know that every time I talked to you about this book, nothing made sense. Thanks for listening to me anyways and turning up Radiohead right after.

Thanks to my mom, Rebecca Mlinek, for your eternal patience, compassion, and empathy. I don't know how you do it.

Huge thanks to Mrs. Supplee, without whom this book would not be possible. Your mentorship and guidance not only shaped me into a better writer, but into a kinder person, and for that I cannot thank you enough.

Finally, my most special thanks to the Literary Arts Class of 2017. You guys are the turtles who hold up the world. I give all my love to you.

AUTHOR'S BIOGRAPHY

Katie Mlinek is a writer and filmmaker from Baltimore, Maryland. She is the oldest of six girls and spends her days fighting for food, writing, forcing everyone she knows to watch great movies, and making films. She has won Best Narrative Short at three film festivals, including the Film Now International Film Festival, and has been an official selection in the likes of the Santa Monica Teen Beach Film Festival and All American HS Film Fest, among others. She has been previously published in the *Synergy*, Carver Center's Literary Magazine, and Scholastic's *2016 Best Teen Writing* anthology. She will be attending the UNC School of the Arts for filmmaking in the fall of 2017.

Made in the USA
Lexington, KY
04 May 2017